BEACH BREAKS: SHORT SURF STORIES

Ripples of Adventure: Surfing Tales from Beach Breaks

Elle

THE WAVE WHISPERER

In a quaint coastal town nestled between rocky cliffs and sun-kissed beaches, there lived a young man named Jake. From the very moment he entered this world, he was captivated by the mesmerizing rhythm of the ocean. The gentle lull of the waves and the distant cries of seagulls felt like a soothing lullaby to his young soul. As he grew, his fascination with the sea only deepened, and the ocean's call became a permanent echo in his heart.

Jake's family had been fishermen for generations, casting their nets into the deep blue expanse every day to bring home the ocean's bounty. Yet, despite this tradition, Jake's destiny lay elsewhere. While his siblings eagerly embraced the family trade, Jake couldn't shake the feeling that there was more to the sea than fish.

The townsfolk often saw Jake perched on the rocky cliffs, his gaze fixated on the horizon where the surfers danced upon the waves. Their silhouettes, graceful and effortless, seemed like mythical beings to him. The way they glided across the water left him in awe, and he couldn't help but dream of joining their ranks.

However, Jake's family lacked the means to purchase a surfboard, and his parents couldn't afford to indulge his dreams. Undeterred, he fashioned makeshift boards from driftwood and spent countless hours perfecting the art of balance and rhythm. With unwavering determination, he honed his skills on the waves, learning to read the ocean's temperamental moods.

One bright morning, as the sun cast a golden sheen upon the water, Jake's life took a fateful turn. He ventured closer to the beach to observe the surfers up close when he spotted an old, weathered man riding the waves with the grace of a master. His name was Hank, a legendary surfer who had traveled the world, conquering the most challenging waves.

Hank noticed the young dreamer watching him with wide-eyed wonder. He paddled over to Jake and, with a weathered smile, said, "You've got the heart of a surfer, kid. Want to learn the ways of the sea?"

Jake couldn't believe his luck. It was as if destiny itself had sent Hank to him. With Hank as his mentor, Jake's surfing journey began. They spent countless hours in the water, with Hank imparting his wisdom and Jake absorbing every lesson like a sponge. He learned to read the waves, anticipate their movements, and understand the ocean's language.

As the days turned into weeks and the weeks into months, Jake's skills improved by leaps and bounds. He was no longer content with makeshift boards; Hank gifted him a proper surfboard, one that seemed to have a piece of Hank's soul in it. With each sunrise and sunset, Jake's confidence grew, and his love for the waves deepened.

Soon, the townspeople noticed the young surfer, who had once watched from the sidelines, now gracefully riding the waves. They called him the "Wave Whisperer" because of his seemingly mystical connection to the ocean.

With newfound fame came new challenges. Tourists flocked to

the coastal town to witness the Wave Whisperer's incredible feats on the water. Jake became a local legend, and the pressure to perform grew with each passing day. Yet, with Hank's guidance and his unyielding passion for the ocean, Jake was always up for the challenge.

But the ultimate test awaited him—the legendary Big Kahuna, a colossal wave that had crushed the spirits of even the bravest surfers for generations. To be considered a true surfer, Jake knew he had to conquer this behemoth.

One bright morning, the sun painted the sky in shades of orange and pink, a sign of the impending challenge. Jake and Hank, a dynamic duo of youth and experience, paddled out to face the Big Kahuna. The waves were relentless, and the ocean roared, challenging them at every turn. Fear was a distant memory for Jake, who had become one with the sea.

As they approached the colossal wave, Jake could hear Hank's voice in his head, guiding him, "It's just water, Jake. Respect it, and it will respect you."

With one final, powerful stroke, Jake turned his board toward the wave, aligning himself with destiny. The moment was perfect, the wave surging beneath him. He rose to his feet, his heart racing, and a grin on his face that matched the sun's brilliance.

He rode the Big Kahuna, a fearless surfer in perfect harmony with the ocean's might. The town cheered from the shore as Jake conquered the legendary wave, solidifying his status as a true legend.

From that day forward, Jake continued to ride the waves, becoming an inspiration to countless others who dreamt of the sea. He had found his place, where he truly belonged, riding the waves of destiny. And so, his story spread, a tale of determination, mentorship, and the undeniable call of the ocean, inspiring generations of surfers to follow their hearts and ride the waves of their dreams.

In the wake of his triumphant conquest of the Big Kahuna, Jake's life transformed into a whirlwind of interviews, sponsorships, and invitations to surf on some of the world's most renowned waves. The once-hidden gem of a coastal town became a surfing hotspot, attracting enthusiasts and professionals alike.

Amidst the newfound fame, Jake remained grounded, his heart forever tethered to the waves that had cradled his dreams. The local surf shop, once struggling to stay afloat, now thrived under the "Wave Whisperer" brand. Jake collaborated with the shop to design his own line of surfboards, each one infused with the spirit of the ocean. The profits were shared with the community, supporting local initiatives and preserving the coastal environment that had shaped Jake's destiny.

Hank, though content to remain in the shadows, reveled in the success of his protégé. The old surfer found joy in imparting wisdom to the next generation, fostering a legacy that transcended the limits of time. Jake, in turn, became a mentor to young surfers, paying forward the guidance he had received from Hank.

As the years unfolded, the coastal town underwent a metamorphosis. Surfing schools emerged, and the rhythmic dance of surfers on the waves became a symbol of the town's resilience and adaptability. The once quaint community embraced the influx of visitors, weaving together a tapestry of diverse cultures united by a shared love for the sea.

Jake's journey also took him to distant shores, where he

discovered new waves and forged connections with surfers from around the globe. Yet, no matter where he traveled, his heart always longed for the familiar embrace of his hometown waves. He found solace in the fact that, no matter how vast the ocean, its language remained universal.

One day, as Jake stood on a foreign shore, a letter arrived, weathered and adorned with stamps from his coastal town. It was a heartfelt invitation from the town's mayor, requesting his presence for the inaugural "Wave Whisperer Festival." The event aimed to celebrate the town's transformation, with surf competitions, environmental initiatives, and a gathering of surf enthusiasts from all walks of life.

Touched by the invitation, Jake returned to his roots, greeted by the familiar sights and sounds that had shaped his childhood. The festival unfolded like a symphony of joy, with the waves as the conductor and surfers as the instruments. The town, once secluded, now stood as a testament to the transformative power of following one's passion.

During the festival, a young boy approached Jake, wide-eyed and eager to learn. His dreams mirrored those of Jake's youth, and the seasoned surfer saw a reflection of himself in the boy's gaze. With a smile, Jake handed the young dreamer a surfboard, passing on the legacy that had been entrusted to him by Hank.

The festival marked the beginning of an annual tradition, a homage to the sea and the unyielding spirit of those who rode its waves. The coastal town, now known as the Surfing Sanctuary, became a sanctuary not only for surfers but for dreamers and wanderers seeking a connection with something greater than themselves.

As the sun dipped below the horizon, casting hues of orange and pink across the water, Jake stood on the rocky cliffs, a silhouette against the fading light. The ocean whispered its eternal secrets, and in that moment, Jake knew that his journey had come full circle. The waves, once a distant melody, now echoed in the hearts of all those who had dared to chase their dreams.

The legacy of the Wave Whisperer lived on, not just in the stories told around campfires or the surfboards bearing his name, but in the undying spirit of a coastal town that had embraced the call of the ocean. And as the night unfolded, the waves continued their timeless dance, a symphony that resonated with the dreams of those who dared to listen.

GUARDIANS OF THE WAVES: UNVEILLING AZURE BAY SURFING SECRETS

Detective Amelia Waters stood on the sandy shores of Azure Bay, her sharp eyes scanning the horizon. The small coastal town had always been a haven for surfers seeking the perfect wave, but today, the waves whispered a different tale—a tale of mystery and intrigue that beckoned Amelia into the heart of the ocean.

It all began with the disappearance of Jake Turner, a renowned surfer and the pride of Azure Bay. Known for his fearless approach to the waves, Jake had gone missing under mysterious circumstances. The townsfolk were baffled, and rumours of foul play spread like wildfire through the tight-knit community.
Amelia, a seasoned detective with a passion for the sea, couldn't resist the call of the ocean's mysteries. With a surfboard tucked under her arm and determination in her eyes, she set out to unravel the enigma surrounding Jake's disappearance.

The first stop on her investigation was the local surf shack, a hub of activity where surfers gathered to discuss the latest swells and share tales of their daring exploits. As Amelia entered the rustic wooden building, the salty scent of the sea filled her nostrils. Surfers exchanged knowing glances, their expressions a mix of concern and curiosity.

"Detective Waters," greeted Finn Harper, a weathered surfer with a perpetual tan. "You're here about Jake, aren't you?"

Amelia nodded, "That's right, Finn. Mind filling me in on the details? Where was he last seen?"

Finn scratched his head, his gaze distant as he recalled the events leading up to Jake's disappearance. "Last I saw him, he caught a massive wave near the cliffs. It was like he was one with the ocean. But then, poof, he vanished. No one knows what happened after that."

Amelia's investigative instincts kicked into high gear. She questioned other surfers, piecing together a timeline of Jake's last surf session. As she listened to their accounts, a pattern emerged—a pattern that led her to believe that something more than a mere accident was at play.

She headed to the cliffs where Jake had last been seen, the crashing waves below providing a rhythmic backdrop to her thoughts. The cliffside offered a vantage point that revealed the vastness of the ocean and the secrets it held. As Amelia surveyed the scene, a glint of something caught her eye—something metallic embedded in the rocks.

With careful steps, she approached the mysterious object. It was a surfboard, unmistakably Jake's, wedged between the rocks as if tossed there by a powerful force. Amelia examined it closely, noting scratches and dents that hinted at a struggle.

Determined to delve deeper, Amelia enlisted the help of a local marine biologist, Dr. Emily Mitchell. Together, they explored the underwater caves near the cliffs, searching for any clues that might shed light on Jake's disappearance. The ocean floor, adorned with vibrant corals and teeming with marine life, held secrets that awaited discovery.

In the depths of a cave, they found an anomaly—an ancient chest, covered in barnacles and seemingly untouched by the passage of time. Amelia's detective instincts tingled, and with Dr. Mitchell's expertise, they carefully retrieved the chest and brought it to the surface.

As they pried open the centuries-old chest, a collection of weathered scrolls and artifacts spilled out. Among them was a map, intricately detailing the underwater topography of Azure Bay and marking a location that coincided with the mysterious disappearance of Jake Turner.

Amelia studied the map, her mind racing with possibilities. The ocean, it seemed, held not only the key to Jake's fate but also a long-buried secret that could reshape the town's history. With newfound determination, she embarked on an underwater expedition, armed with the ancient map as her guide.

The underwater journey led Amelia to a hidden cavern, its entrance concealed by the ebb and flow of the tides. As she swam deeper into the dark abyss, phosphorescent sea creatures illuminated her path. The cavern opened into a vast chamber, where the water seemed to shimmer with an otherworldly glow.

Amelia's gaze fell upon a mesmerizing sight—a field of bioluminescent algae that danced with the currents. In the centre of the chamber stood a colossal statue, its features weathered by centuries beneath the sea. The statue depicted a figure with outstretched arms, cradling a surfboard.

Driven by a hunch, Amelia examined the statue closely. In the hands of the ancient figure, she discovered an inscription that spoke of a guardian of the waves—a protector whose duty was to maintain the balance between the ocean and the land.

The legend hinted at a powerful artifact hidden within the depths —a relic that bestowed unimaginable abilities upon those who possessed it. Amelia's detective instincts told her that Jake's disappearance was intricately tied to this ancient power, and she resolved to uncover the truth.

With the help of a skilled underwater archaeologist, Amelia delved into the secrets of the submerged cavern. As they unearthed relics and deciphered ancient inscriptions, a tale of an ancient brotherhood emerged—a group of surfers who had harnessed the ocean's energy to protect their town from external threats.

The artifacts within the cavern revealed that Jake Turner, unwittingly or not, had become the latest guardian of the waves. The surfboard he wielded possessed a connection to the ancient power, and its disappearance had disrupted the delicate balance that the brotherhood had maintained for centuries.

As Amelia pieced together the puzzle, a new threat emerged. A rival group, aware of the ancient power hidden within Azure Bay, sought to exploit it for their gain. Led by a shadowy figure known only as Blackwater, they aimed to seize control of the artifact and wield its power for nefarious purposes.

Amelia, now armed with the knowledge of the ocean's ancient guardians, raced against time to prevent a catastrophe. She enlisted the help of Finn Harper and other surfers who, upon learning of the town's hidden history, embraced their roles as protectors of the waves.

The final confrontation unfolded at the heart of the submerged cavern, where the ancient artifact pulsed with energy. Blackwater and his followers, armed with knowledge stolen from the scrolls, descended upon the chamber, ready to claim the power for themselves.

A fierce battle ensued beneath the waves, the clash of surfboards and the roar of the ocean echoing through the cavern. Amelia, Finn, and the surfers fought bravely, determined to uphold the legacy of the ancient brotherhood and safeguard the town from the looming threat.

Amelia found herself face to face with Blackwater. The mysterious figure, clad in dark attire that seemed to absorb the very essence of the ocean, wielded a surfboard infused with dark energy. His intent was clear—to harness the power of the artifact and bend the ocean to his will.
Amelia, drawing upon the strength of the ancient guardians, faced Blackwater in a high-stakes surf-off. The waves, manipulated by the power of the artifact, surged and crashed around them. The fate of Azure Bay hung in the balance as the two surfers engaged in a duel that transcended the physical realm.

In the midst of the battle, the ancient guardian statue came to life, its eyes glowing with a radiant intensity. The spirit of the long-forgotten protector merged with Amelia, infusing her with the wisdom and strength of centuries. Empowered by this spectral alliance, she confronted Blackwater with unwavering determination.

Amelia and Blackwater rode the tumultuous waves, their surfboards carving through the water with unparalleled skill. The ocean itself seemed to respond to their every move, as if the ancient power contested between light and darkness, between the guardians and those who sought to exploit the sea's magic.

The battle reached its climax in a colossal wave that surged towards the cavern's entrance. Amelia and Blackwater, caught in the grip of the swirling current, faced a choice—to succumb to the overpowering force or to harness the very essence of the ocean to emerge victorious.
Amelia closed her eyes, drawing upon the wisdom of the ancient

guardian within her. In that moment of connection, she felt the heartbeat of the ocean, the eons of knowledge it held, and the collective strength of the brotherhood of surfers who had come before her. With a surge of determination, she channelled this energy into her surfboard, transforming it into a beacon of light that cut through the darkness.

As the colossal wave crashed upon them, the clash of light and dark energy illuminated the cavern. The waters roared, echoing the fierce battle between the guardians and Blackwater's followers. When the tumult subsided, Amelia found herself standing on the ocean floor, the artifact pulsating with a renewed brilliance beside her.

Blackwater, defeated and disoriented, emerged from the water. The dark energy that had surrounded him had dissipated, leaving only a sense of emptiness. The power he sought to control had rejected him, recognizing the purity of Amelia's intent and the collective spirit of the guardians.

In the aftermath, as the surfers and the town gathered on the shore, a sense of peace settled over Azure Bay. The ancient artifact, now stabilized by the guardians' united front, radiated a gentle glow that spread through the ocean. The waves, once tumultuous, now lapped at the shore with a soothing rhythm.

Amelia, weary but victorious, stood on the sandy beach. The town that had been on the brink of disaster was now bathed in a newfound harmony. The surfers, once unaware of their legacy, embraced their role as guardians of the waves, vowing to protect the ancient power that lay beneath the ocean's surface.

In the days that followed, Azure Bay transformed. The surfers and the townsfolk worked together to preserve the delicate balance between the ocean and the land. The brotherhood of guardians, once a secret whispered among the waves, became a source of pride for the community.

Amelia, having unravelled the mystery of Jake's disappearance and the ancient brotherhood, found a new connection to the sea. She continued to patrol the shores, not only as a detective but as a guardian of the waves, ensuring that the town remained in harmony with the ocean's magic.

As time passed, the legend of Azure Bay's guardians spread beyond the town's borders. Surfers from distant shores sought the thrill of riding the waves that held a touch of ancient power. Azure Bay became a beacon for those who understood the delicate dance between the surfers and the sea.

Finn Harper, once a seasoned surfer seeking the ultimate thrill, became a leader among the guardians. He trained a new generation of surfers, imparting the wisdom passed down from centuries past. The surf shack, once a gathering place for tales of daring exploits, now served as a training ground for those who embraced their role as protectors of the waves.

The ancient artifact, housed in a protective chamber deep within the submerged cavern, continued to pulse with energy. It became a symbol of the town's resilience and a reminder of the unity forged between the surfers and the ocean. The legends of Azure Bay's guardians echoed through time, a testament to the enduring connection between the sea and those who dared to ride its waves.

And so, Azure Bay thrived as a coastal haven where the mysteries of the ocean intertwined with the courage of those who surfed its waves. Detective Amelia Waters, now a guardian in her own right, stood on the shores, gazing out at the horizon with a sense of fulfilment. The ocean, once a canvas of mystery and intrigue, now flowed in harmony with the guardians who had unlocked its secrets.

THE HARMONY OF TIDES

Once upon a time, in the small coastal town of Cresthaven, there lived a young surfer named Alex. With sun-kissed hair and a perpetual tan, Alex's love for the ocean was as boundless as the waves that crashed along the shore. From dawn till dusk, the rhythmic sound of the surf echoed in Alex's heart, calling for a dance upon the crests of the mighty sea.
Cresthaven was known for its legendary surf spot, a point break named Neptune's Grace. Surfers from far and wide flocked to Cresthaven to challenge the waves and earn their stripes. Alex had grown up watching the seasoned surfers conquer Neptune's Grace, dreaming of the day when those waves would bow before them.

One fateful morning, as the sun painted the sky with hues of pink and gold, Alex stood at the water's edge, surfboard in hand, ready to embark on an adventure. The sea whispered secrets, promising a day of unparalleled waves. This was the day Alex had been waiting for—the day to surf Neptune's Grace.

As Alex paddled out, the waves grew taller, their energy palpable. The salty breeze mingled with the adrenaline in the air. The first wave approached, a colossal wall of water, and Alex felt a surge of both fear and excitement. With a swift pop-up, Alex rode the wave with grace, dancing along its powerful rhythm. The crowd on the shore erupted in cheers as Alex carved through the water, a master of Neptune's Grace.

As the day unfolded, Alex surfed wave after wave, each ride more thrilling than the last. The sun climbed higher in the sky, casting a golden glow upon the sea. It seemed as though Neptune himself was orchestrating a symphony of waves to honour this exceptional surfer.

Amidst the cheers and applause, Alex noticed a mysterious figure on the shore—a weathered old man with eyes that mirrored the depths of the ocean. The old man approached, a knowing smile on his face.

"Your connection with the sea is remarkable, young one," he said. "But remember, the ocean is both a friend and a teacher. Respect its power, and it will unveil its secrets to you."

With those cryptic words, the old man vanished into the crowd, leaving Alex to ponder the deeper meaning behind them. Eager to explore the ocean's teachings, Alex continued to ride the waves, embracing the challenge and embracing the serenity that the sea offered.

As the day waned and the sun began its descent, painting the sky with fiery hues, a massive set approached—the kind that surfers spoke of in hushed tones. The crowd fell silent, anticipating the grand finale. Alex's heart raced, feeling the pulse of the ocean beneath.

With unwavering determination, Alex paddled into the looming wave, a wall of liquid power ready to engulf everything in its path. The drop was steep, and for a moment, time seemed to stand still. But Alex rode the wave with a perfect blend of skill and intuition, a harmonious dance with Neptune's Grace.

As the wave rolled towards the shore, Alex emerged from the spray, triumphant. The crowd erupted into applause, and even the ocean seemed to clap in approval. The mysterious old man reappeared, his eyes filled with pride.

"You have learned well, young one," he said. "The ocean has accepted you into its embrace. Carry its teachings with you, and you will forever be a master of Neptune's Grace."

From that day forward, Alex became a legend in Cresthaven, a surfer whose connection with the sea went beyond skill—it was a spiritual dance with the waves. As the sun dipped below the horizon, casting the world in shades of twilight, Alex stood on the shore, grateful for the lessons learned and the endless waves that awaited, always ready to share the dance with Neptune's Grace.

As the seasons changed, Alex continued to surf Neptune's Grace, becoming a beacon for aspiring surfers seeking not just the thrill of the ride, but a deeper connection with the ocean. The mysterious old man revealed to be a wise sage named Kairos, became a mentor to Alex, sharing ancient tales of the sea and its profound wisdom.

Under Kairos's guidance, Alex explored new dimensions of surfing, delving into the spiritual aspects of the sport. Together, they would paddle out before dawn, communing with the ocean in its quietude. They would sit on their boards, feeling the ebb and flow of the waves, exchanging stories with the seagulls that soared overhead.
Cresthaven became a haven for surfers seeking not only the physical challenge of Neptune's Grace but also the soul-stirring experience that Alex embodied. The town buzzed with a unique energy, a blend of the sea's power and the spiritual resonance that emanated from those who embraced its teachings.

One day, a stranger arrived in Cresthaven—a surfer with a haunted look in their eyes, seeking solace in the waves. Alex, sensing the inner turmoil, approached with empathy. The stranger, named Maya, spoke of a turbulent past and a quest for redemption through the dance with Neptune's Grace.

Alex, recalling Kairos's words, became a guide for Maya, introducing them to the ancient rituals of surfing. Together, they paddled out into the predawn stillness, sharing stories of resilience and renewal. As they caught waves side by side, transformative energy enveloped Maya, and the weight of their past seemed to dissipate into the vastness of the ocean.

Word spread of this transformative surfing experience, drawing more seekers to Cresthaven. The town evolved into a community of kindred spirits, bound by their love for the sea and a shared journey of self-discovery. Alex, now not just a surfer but a spiritual leader, embraced the role with humility, always attributing their wisdom to the ocean and the teachings passed down by Kairos.

As the years passed, Cresthaven thrived as a unique surfing destination, attracting individuals from all walks of life. The town became a melting pot of cultures and backgrounds, united by the universal language of the waves. Neptune's Grace, once a challenging break reserved for the fearless, now embraced surfers of all levels, each finding their rhythm in the dance of the sea.

One day, as Alex stood on the shore, watching the sun dip below the horizon, Kairos appeared one last time. With a nod of approval, Kairos conveyed that the time had come for Alex to pass on the mantle—to guide the next generation of surfers and continue the legacy of Neptune's Grace.

With a grateful heart, Alex accepted the responsibility, knowing that the cycle of learning, teaching, and surfing would endure. As the sun dipped below the horizon, casting a warm glow over the ocean, Alex took a final glance at Neptune's Grace, ready to share its timeless teachings with those who would follow in their footsteps.

And so, the tale of Cresthaven continued, a town where the sea whispered its secrets to those who listened, and the dance with Neptune's Grace became a journey of the soul.

ETERNAL TIDES: A LOVE STORY IN PACIFIC HAVEN

The seasons changed, and with them, Pacific Haven transformed into a canvas of colors. Autumn brought a gentle breeze, and the town adorned itself with a palette of warm hues. Jake and Lily's love, like the changing leaves, evolved with a quiet grace. They navigated the ebb and flow of life, building a foundation sturdy as the coastal cliffs that framed their world.

As winter descended, the town embraced a quiet solitude. The waves, though still and tranquil, held the promise of a vibrant spring. Jake and Lily, bundled up in cozy scarves, strolled along the deserted beach, their footprints leaving imprints in the damp sand. Neptune, temporarily retired, stood guard against the winter winds, patiently awaiting the return of warmer days.

It was during these winter nights, by the crackling fire in their beachside cottage, that Jake and Lily dreamt of the future. Together, they crafted plans as intricate as the seashell necklace that adorned Lily's neck. Jake's surfing aspirations merged seamlessly with Lily's artistic pursuits, creating a vision of a life intertwined with passion and purpose.

Spring breathed life back into Pacific Haven, and with it, a renewed energy surged through Jake and Lily. Neptune, dusted off and waxed with care, once again became the vessel that carried them into the embrace of the ocean. They surfed under the blossoming cherry blossoms, a celebration of love and resilience that mirrored the rebirth of nature.

Amidst the blooming flowers and longer days, Jake proposed to Lily on a cliff overlooking the vast expanse of the sea. The setting sun painted the sky with hues of pink and gold as he knelt down, seashell necklace in hand. With tears of joy and the crashing waves as their witnesses, Lily said yes, sealing their commitment beneath the ever-watchful gaze of the Pacific.

Their love story continued to unfold, chapters written in the golden sands of summer. They hosted beach bonfires, where laughter mingled with the crackling flames, and shared secrets under the starlit sky. Pacific Haven, once a backdrop to their beginning, became a stage for the adventures they crafted together.

As the years passed, Jake and Lily faced the inevitable challenges of life—storms that tested their resilience and calms that allowed for introspection. Yet, through it all, their love remained a constant, an anchor in the ever-changing sea of existence.

Neptune, weathered and adorned with countless memories, became a symbol of their journey. It stood proudly in their living room, a reminder of the waves conquered and the storms weathered. Each ding and scratch told a story—a testament to their shared experiences, the highs and lows etched into its fiberglass surface.

Together, they witnessed the passage of time like the rhythmic rise and fall of the tides. In the warmth of their beachside home, surrounded by the echoes of laughter and the scent of salt in the air, Jake and Lily embraced the beauty of a love that had weathered the seasons.

And so, as the sun dipped below the horizon once again, casting a kaleidoscope of colors over the Pacific, Jake and Lily stood on the beach, hand in hand. The waves, a constant companion throughout their journey, whispered tales of a love that had become as eternal as the ocean itself.

Pacific Haven, a witness to their love story, held the echoes of their laughter, the imprints of their footprints, and the promise of countless sunsets yet to be shared. For Jake and Lily, the journey was not just about riding the waves—it was about navigating life's currents together, hand in hand, into the endless horizon of their shared destiny.

TEMPEST'S EMBRACE: SURFING THE SECRETS OF MAVERICK'S

In the heart of the vast Pacific, where the horizon melded seamlessly with the sky and the ocean's depths concealed untold mysteries, a gripping surfing thriller unfolded its tale.

Meet Alex, a formidable surfer with an insatiable thirst for adrenaline and a past veiled in shadows that clung to their every move. Drawn by an irresistible pull to the enigmatic allure of Maverick's, a legendary surf spot notorious for its colossal waves and unpredictable currents, Alex embarked on a quest to conquer the ocean's untamed fury.

The journey began on a windswept morning, the scent of salt in the air as Alex approached Maverick's with a weathered surfboard named Tempest. The waves, towering like titans of the sea, crashed against the coastal cliffs, creating a symphony of power that echoed through the shores. Maverick's, with its reputation as a proving ground for the bravest surfers, cast an imposing shadow over the surfing world.

As Alex delved into the world of big-wave surfing, a series of mysterious incidents and disappearances rocked the tight-knit surfing community. Whispers of a legendary sea creature, tales passed down through generations, circulated among the surfers, adding an eerie layer to the already treacherous waves.

Determined to uncover the truth, Alex became entangled in a web of conspiracy, betrayal, and the dark forces that lurked beneath the ocean's surface.

Haunted by recurring visions of a ghostly figure beckoning from the depths, Alex sought solace in the waves, the rhythmic dance of the ocean offering both refuge and uncertainty. The line between reality and the supernatural blurred with each surf session, leading to heart-pounding encounters with both the natural and paranormal forces that ruled the sea.

In the pursuit of answers, Alex formed an unlikely alliance with Dr. Maya Rodriguez, a marine biologist whose expertise extended from the scientific intricacies of the ocean to the uncharted realms of folklore and myth. Together, they navigated the intricate dance between human ambition and the primal power of the ocean, racing against time to expose the truth before Maverick's claimed its next victim.

The novel unfolded against the backdrop of thrilling surf competitions, where each wave became a battleground between survival and the relentless allure of the abyss. Amidst the crashing waves and echoing roars of the ocean, Alex grappled with personal demons and faced the ultimate challenge—riding the monstrous wave that guarded the secrets of Maverick's.

As the tension rose, Maverick's revealed its secrets slowly, like the unveiling of an ancient manuscript. The surfing community, once a tightly-knit brotherhood, now found itself divided between those who sought the thrill of conquering the unknown and those who feared the consequences of awakening the supernatural forces that lay dormant beneath the waves.

In a pulse-pounding climax, Alex confronted the supernatural force that had haunted their every move, unraveling a tapestry of ancient myths and modern-day conspiracies. The ocean, a relentless adversary and a faithful ally, became the stage for a showdown between human courage and the elemental forces that shaped destiny.

As the final wave crashed, and the truth emerged from the depths, Alex found redemption in the embrace of the sea. The surfing thriller concluded with a sense of closure, yet the ocean's mysteries lingered, inviting future surfers to brave the waves and explore the enigmatic depths that echoed with the tales of those who dared to challenge the untamed majesty of the Pacific.

In the aftermath, the surfing community grappled with the revelation, and Maverick's, once a symbol of conquest, became a haunting reminder of the delicate balance between human ambition and the primal forces that governed the ocean. Alex, forever changed by the ordeal, chose to continue riding the waves, not as a conqueror but as a guardian of the ocean's secrets.

The epilogue unfolded against the backdrop of a serene sunset, the waves lapping gently against the shore. Alex, surfboard in hand, gazed out at the horizon, a reflection of both triumph and humility in their eyes. The legacy of Maverick's lived on, not just in the lore of surfing but in the collective memory of those who dared to challenge the boundaries of the known.

As the stars emerged in the velvety sky, casting their shimmering glow over the ocean, Alex walked away from Maverick's, leaving footprints in the sand that would be washed away by the tide. The ocean, eternal and enigmatic, held its secrets close, inviting the next generation of surfers to embark on their own quests, to ride the waves and uncover the mysteries that awaited beneath the surface. And so, the legend of Maverick's continued, an indelible mark on the canvas of the vast and unpredictable Pacific.

THE SURFING DETECTIVE

Detective Alex Rivers, renowned for his unconventional investigative methods, had always found solace in the rhythmic dance of the ocean waves. The salty breeze, the sound of seagulls, and the call of distant surfboards became his sanctuary amidst the chaos of city life. Little did he know that his love for the sea would intertwine with his next enigma—one that would unfold along the sun-kissed shores of Crescent Cove.

It all began on a misty morning when a weathered surfboard washed ashore, adorned with symbols that seemed to whisper ancient secrets. Alex, drawn to the mystique of the ocean, caught wind of the discovery and felt a curious pull as if the waves themselves were urging him to uncover the story behind the cryptic surfboard.

As he arrived at Crescent Cove, the surfing community greeted him with a mixture of scepticism and curiosity. They were a tight-knit tribe, bonded by their love for the sea, and the arrival of an outsider, especially one bearing the title of detective, stirred both interest and wariness.

The surfboard, now a centrepiece of the local surf shop, became Alex's focal point. Its symbols, a blend of tribal patterns and celestial imagery, hinted at a narrative that transcended the ordinary. The detective, with a surfboard rental in hand, ventured into the ocean, allowing the waves to guide him towards the heart of the mystery.

As Alex paddled through the undulating waters, he observed the surfers around him, each carving their own stories into the waves. The ocean, with its timeless ebb and flow, seemed to be the keeper of secrets—a silent witness to the comings and goings of the surfing community.
The detective's investigation led him to the heart of Crescent Cove's surf culture. He befriended locals at beachside bonfires, shared laughter over shared waves, and gradually earned the trust of the coastal dwellers.

Alongside the surfers, Alex learned the nuances of wave-riding, gaining insights into the unspoken code that governed the surfing world.
However, beneath the camaraderie and the crashing waves, Alex sensed an undercurrent of tension. Cryptic messages began to surface, anonymous threats directed at surfers who seemed to excel a little too much in competitions or gain a bit too much recognition. The paradise of Crescent Cove was starting to show cracks, and Alex knew there was more at stake than the tranquillity of the surf.

One fateful afternoon, as the sun dipped low on the horizon, Alex witnessed a heated confrontation between two surfers, Mark and Elena. Their exchange, laced with accusations and resentment, hinted at a deeper conflict simmering beneath the surface. The detective's instincts flared, recognizing the potential link between the surfboard symbols, the mysterious messages, and the brewing animosity within the community.

That night, Alex's investigative journey took an unexpected turn. A bonfire gathering, usually a celebration of the day's surfing conquests, turned into a scene of chaos as someone slashed the surfboards left unattended. The detective, attuned to the pulse of the ocean, caught a glimpse of a shadowy figure disappearing into the night.

Determined to uncover the truth, Alex gave chase, his footsteps echoing the urgency of the crashing waves. The pursuit led him to a secluded cove, where he discovered a makeshift shelter crafted from driftwood and tattered tarps. The remnants of broken surfboards, torn wetsuits, and the chilling discovery of a blood-stained blade painted a haunting tableau—a crime scene hidden within the beauty of Crescent Cove.

As Alex stood in the cove, the ocean seemed to hold its breath, as if awaiting the detective's next move. The symbols on the mysterious surfboard, the escalating tensions among the surfers, and the evidence of a crime converged into a puzzle that begged to be solved. Crescent Cove, once a haven of serenity, had transformed into the backdrop for a mystery that would test Alex's detective skills and the resilience of a surfing community bound by more than just the love of the sea.

As Detective Alex Rivers stood in the secluded cove, surrounded by the remnants of shattered surfboards and the ominous presence of a blood-stained blade, he felt the weight of the mystery pressing upon him. The waves, once a soothing melody, seemed to murmur secrets that danced just beyond the edge of his understanding.

The morning after the discovery, the surfing community awoke to the news of the crime scene, and a palpable tension gripped Crescent Cove. The bonfire gatherings became hushed, and the surfers exchanged wary glances, questioning the once-unquestionable bond that held them together.

Elena, the surfer whose confrontation with Mark had caught Alex's attention, became the focal point of the investigation. The symbols on the surfboard, the anonymous threats, and the confrontation now painted a picture that seemed to point in her direction. As Alex delved deeper into her past, he uncovered a tale of betrayal and revenge—a narrative woven into the very fabric of Crescent Cove's surfing history.

However, just as the pieces of the puzzle seemed to align, an unexpected twist threw the investigation into disarray. The detective, meticulously retracing the events leading to the crime, discovered a hidden alcove beneath the cliffs—an alcove that harboured not only discarded surfboards and wetsuits but also a stash of incriminating evidence.

Among the items hidden in the alcove was a second surfboard, identical to the one found washed ashore. The symbols, the carvings, and the enigmatic patterns mirrored the original, raising unsettling questions. It was as if Crescent Cove had become a stage for a meticulously crafted performance, and the detective found himself caught in the crosscurrents of a grand deception.

The unexpected revelation shifted the focus of the investigation. The surfboard once believed to hold the key to the mystery, now emerged as a mere pawn in a more elaborate game. The anonymous threats, the confrontations, and the atmosphere of paranoia took on new dimensions as Alex grappled with the realization that the true mastermind remained hidden among the surfers.

As the detective confronted the surfing community with the revelation, suspicions ran high. Friendships that had weathered the waves now faced the turbulent currents of doubt. The unexpected twist not only deepened the mystery but also threatened to unravel the very fabric of trust that held Crescent Cove's surfing tribe together.

Amid the turmoil, an unlikely ally emerged—Max, the surfer who had discovered the original surfboard. Max, once a symbol of the community's suspicion, revealed that he, too, had stumbled upon the hidden alcove. His motive, however, was not deception but a genuine desire to expose the truth and restore harmony to the waves they all loved.

Together, Alex and Max embarked on a new phase of the investigation, unravelling the threads of the grand deception that had woven its way through Crescent Cove. The hidden alcove, once a chamber of secrets, became the nexus of their efforts, revealing a complex network of rivalries, alliances, and personal vendettas that extended far beyond the shoreline.

As the detective and the surfer delved into the heart of the mystery, they uncovered a plot to manipulate the surfing community—a scheme orchestrated by an outsider with a vendetta against the surfers of Crescent Cove. The true puppeteer, it seemed, had skillfully played the role of puppet, using the surfboard symbols and the escalating tensions to sow discord and chaos.

In a dramatic revelation, the outsider was unmasked—a disgraced former surfing champion seeking revenge for perceived slights that had driven them away from the community years ago. The motive, while rooted in personal grievances, had taken on a grander scale, as the outsider sought to disrupt the serenity of Crescent Cove as a form of twisted retribution.

As the truth emerged, the surfing community grappled with the realization that the enemy was not among them but an external force that had infiltrated their haven. The waves, once witnesses to deception, now seemed to applaud the resilience and unity displayed by Crescent Cove's surfers in the face of an unexpected adversary.

"The Surfing Detective" reached its climax as the detective, the surfer, and the community confronted the outsider, exposing their grand deception. The ocean, ever the impartial judge, bore witness to the resolution of a mystery that had tested the bonds of trust and loyalty in Crescent Cove.

The unexpected twist not only redefined the narrative but also reinforced the strength of the surfing community. As the waves carried away the echoes of the outsider's plot, Crescent Cove resumed its role as a sanctuary for surfers, united by a shared love for the sea and a newfound resilience forged through the unexpected currents of deception.

THE SURFING COMPETITION

In the heart of the surfing world, where the sun-kissed shores met the azure embrace of the Pacific, the annual SeaStar Surfing Championship stood as the pinnacle of competition. Surfers from around the globe descended upon the coastal haven of Horizon Bay, where the waves were legendary, and the stakes were higher than the crest of a towering swell.

Meet Jake Thompson, a rising star in the surfing community. With sun-bleached hair and a natural affinity for the ocean, Jake had spent years mastering the art of riding waves. The SeaStar Championship, the most prestigious event in his budding career, beckoned like a siren's call, promising not just glory but a chance to etch his name into the surfing annals.

As the championship's opening ceremony unfolded, Horizon Bay transformed into a vibrant tapestry of colours and energy. The sun painted the sky with hues of pink and gold, casting a warm glow over the sandy beaches and the surfers preparing for the competition. Neptune, Jake's trusty surfboard, stood proudly, waxed to perfection, as the symbol of his journey into the heart of the surfing elite.

The SeaStar Championship was not just a contest of skill; it was a celebration of the surfing culture that bound the community together. Surfers shared stories of triumphs and wipeouts around beach bonfires, their laughter mingling with the rhythmic melody of the waves. In this spirited atmosphere, friendships were forged, and rivalries ignited, creating a dynamic that added an extra layer of excitement to the impending competition.

As the first day of the championship dawned, the ocean seemed to mirror the anticipation in the air. The waves, majestic and relentless, offered a canvas for surfers to paint their stories. Jake, clad in his signature wetsuit, felt the familiar thrill as he paddled into the waiting waves, each swell a reminder of the countless hours of practice that had brought him to this moment.

The initial heats of the SeaStar Championship were a showcase of talent and skill, with surfers executing breathtaking maneuvers that left spectators in awe. Jake navigated the waves with a blend of grace and daring, his every move a testament to the synergy between man and ocean. Neptune, beneath his feet, responded to his commands with an almost sentient understanding.

Amidst the exhilarating rides and the crashing waves, Jake found himself forming unexpected alliances and rivalries. The camaraderie of the surfing community extended beyond the competition, as surfers shared tips, offered encouragement, and, in some cases, engaged in friendly banter that added a touch of drama to the event.

As the sun dipped below the horizon on the first day, the surfers gathered for a beachside celebration. The night was alive with the sounds of laughter and the strumming of guitars, a harmonious melody that resonated with the spirit of the surfing lifestyle. Neptune, adorned with a garland of tropical flowers, stood as a silent witness to the camaraderie that transcended the competition.

Yet, beneath the festive atmosphere, an undercurrent of tension lurked. A rival surfer, Tyler Kane, had emerged as Jake's primary competition. The two surfers, each with their unique style and approach, found themselves on a collision course that promised not just a clash of waves but a battle for supremacy in the surfing world.

The SeaStar Championship, far from being just a series of heats, had evolved into a personal quest for Jake. The waves, once a familiar playground, now represented the ultimate challenge, each swell and break a test of his skill and determination. As he lay under the starlit sky, contemplating the upcoming finals, Jake felt the weight of expectations and the adrenaline of anticipation.

The first part of "The Surfing Competition" concluded with Jake standing on the beach, gazing at the vast expanse of the ocean. The next day held the promise of the finals, where the fate of the championship would be decided. Neptune, gleaming under the moonlight, seemed to whisper words of encouragement, a silent reminder that the journey was far from over.

As Jake closed his eyes, the distant sound of waves crashing against the shore echoed in his mind. The SeaStar Championship had become more than a competition—it was a defining chapter in his surfing odyssey, where every wave carved a piece of his legacy into the ever-shifting sands of Horizon Bay.

The morning of the SeaStar Championship finals arrived with a crescendo of excitement. Horizon Bay, draped in the soft glow of dawn, awaited the showdown between Jake Thompson and Tyler Kane. The rivalry that had simmered beneath the surface now threatened to erupt like a perfectly formed wave crashing against the cliffs.

As Jake prepared for the finals, a sense of focused determination etched on his face, he couldn't shake the lingering tension with Tyler Kane. The origin of their rivalry extended beyond the surf—it echoed the timeless theme of competition spilling into personal realms. A girl named Mia, a free spirit with an infectious love for the ocean, had become the unwitting catalyst for the conflict that now played out on the sunlit shores.

Mia, a fellow surfer with a passion for the waves that rivalled Jake's own, found herself caught in the crosscurrents of the competition. Both Jake and Tyler harboured a growing affection for her, and what had started as friendly banter had evolved into a silent contest for her attention.

The atmosphere on the beach was charged with both the exhilaration of the impending finals and the undercurrents of personal rivalry. Jake, Neptune in hand, tried to focus on the waves that awaited him, but the weight of unresolved emotions lingered in the salty air.

The finals began with the ceremonial paddle-out, surfers forming a circle beyond the break, paying homage to the ocean that had shaped their destinies. Jake and Tyler, side by side yet worlds apart, shared a glance that spoke volumes—a silent agreement that this competition transcended the boundaries of sport.

As the horn blared, signalling the start of the finals, the waves rose to greet the surfers. Jake and Tyler navigated the swells with unparalleled skill, each turn and back a calculated move in the dance of wave-riding mastery. The cheers from the spectators merged with the rhythmic pulse of the ocean, creating a symphony that underscored the intensity of the competition.

Amid the adrenaline-fueled performance, Mia watched from the shore, torn between the two surfers who vied for her affections. The waves, once a source of solace and joy, now mirrored the complexity of human emotions—beautiful yet tumultuous, unpredictable yet captivating.

As the finals progressed, the rivalry between Jake and Tyler reached its zenith. Waves became a battleground, each surfer aiming not just to outmaneuver the other but to claim a victory that extended beyond the realm of the SeaStar Championship. The ocean, a silent witness to their drama, seemed to echo the clash of emotions that unfolded on its surface.

Amidst the high-flying aerials and gravity-defying turns, Jake and Tyler found themselves locked in a fierce exchange. The competition transformed into a duel of wills, a manifestation of the unresolved tension that had simmered beneath the surface. At one point, their boards collided in a tangle of limbs and fibreglass, a physical manifestation of the emotional entanglement that defined their rivalry.

As the final minutes of the competition approached, the tension escalated. The surfers, exhausted yet driven by a relentless pursuit of victory, rode the waves with a fervour that transcended the boundaries of the sport. The beach, once a haven of celebration, now held its breath, the outcome of the finals uncertain.

In a dramatic turn, Jake executed a breathtaking maneuver—a daring tube ride that left spectators in awe. The wave, curling around him like a protective embrace, seemed to carry him towards destiny. The judges, tasked with evaluating the surfers' performance, awarded Jake a near-perfect score, solidifying his position as the SeaStar Champion.

The cheers from the crowd erupted as Jake rode the final wave to the shore, victorious yet acutely aware of the personal toll the competition had taken. Neptune, held high in triumph, bore witness to the culmination of Jake's journey to the top of the surfing world.

As Jake basked in the glory of his victory, the tension that had defined his rivalry with Tyler remained palpable. The surfers, exhausted and emotionally charged, faced each other on the shore. Words were exchanged, accusations hurled, and, in the heat of the moment, a physical altercation ensued.

The fight, fueled by the adrenaline of the competition and the unresolved emotions that had lingered for too long, became a chaotic spectacle on the beach. Fellow surfers and event organizers rushed to intervene, pulling Jake and Tyler apart before the confrontation escalated further. The once-celebratory atmosphere now hung heavy with the weight of discord.

As the dust settled, Jake, bruised but resolute, gazed out at the ocean. The SeaStar Championship, the pinnacle of his surfing career, had come at a cost. The cheers of victory were accompanied by the echoes of personal strife, a reminder that triumphs in the surfing world didn't always translate into victories in the complexities of the heart.

The SeaStar Championship concluded with a bittersweet ambience. Jake, crowned the champion, stood on the podium with Neptune by his side, the trophy a testament to his skill and dedication. Tyler, nursing both physical and emotional wounds, watched from a distance, his eyes reflecting a mixture of defeat and introspection.

Mia, torn between the surfers who had captured her heart in different ways, approached Jake with a congratulatory smile. In that moment of triumph, Jake felt a sense of completeness, a recognition that the waves, though tumultuous, had carried him to a place of personal victory.
As the sun dipped below the horizon, casting a golden glow over the horizon, Jake's victory celebration continued. The beach, a witness to both the triumph and turmoil of the SeaStar Championship, held the imprints of a competition that had

transcended the boundaries of sport and delved into the intricate web of human emotions.

THE TIME-TORN SURFER

Bec, a seasoned surfer with an unquenchable thirst for adventure, found herself standing on the rugged cliffs of 1800s Cornwall, England. The salty breeze carried the echoes of an era long past, and the waves crashing against the rocky shore beckoned her with a siren's call.

In this bygone time, the art of surfing was a hidden gem, known only to a select few who dared to challenge the mighty Atlantic. Bec, equipped with a handmade wooden surfboard, felt the weight of history as she gazed at the untamed waves below. The locals, clad in traditional attire, observed her with a mix of curiosity and scepticism.

Undeterred by the unfamiliar surroundings, Bec descended the cliffs, her surfboard in tow. The cumbersome Victorian attire did little to hinder her determination as she approached the roaring sea. The waves, though formidable, seemed to recognize the surfer's spirit, offering a dance that transcended the boundaries of time.

As Bec paddled into the frigid waters, she became a temporal anomaly—an adventurer from the future embracing the ancient thrill of wave-riding in a world unaccustomed to the sport. The waves, crashing against the rugged coastline, became a canvas for

Bec to paint her story—a tale that unfolded at the intersection of centuries.

Her first ride in Cornwall transported her to a time when the surfboard was a relic, and the ocean was an untamed frontier. The locals, once sceptical, now watched in awe as Bec navigated the waves with a grace that defied the limitations of their understanding. The wooden surfboard, a vessel that bridged the gap between eras, became the symbol of her journey through time.

As the sun dipped below the horizon, Bec, soaked and exhilarated, returned to the cliffs. The locals, their initial skepticism replaced by newfound respect, gathered around, eager to learn the secrets of this enigmatic surfer from a distant future.

In a blink, Bec found herself transported to the futuristic cityscape of Perth. Tall glass buildings stretched towards the sky, reflecting the neon lights that adorned the bustling metropolis. The air hummed with the low thrum of hovercraft, and holographic billboards displayed the latest advancements in technology.

Perth, a city on the cutting edge of progress, had become a playground for surfers who rode waves of light in the virtual realm. Bec, clad in a sleek, tech-infused wetsuit, marvelled at the urban surf parks that dotted the city—a far cry from the rugged cliffs of 1800s Cornwall.

The surfboard in her hand had transformed as well. A futuristic marvel crafted from lightweight materials and embedded with smart technology, it responded to Bec's thoughts and movements with almost intuitive precision. The waves, though digital, offered a unique challenge—a fusion of technology and nature.

As Bec approached the virtual surf park, a holographic interface allowed her to customize the waves. With a flick of her wrist, she conjured waves that mimicked the ferocity of the Atlantic or the tranquility of a tropical lagoon. The surfers around her, equipped with holographic goggles and levitating boards, awaited their turn in this cybernetic surfers' paradise.

The first ride in futuristic Perth was a symphony of light and sound. The waves, a cascade of luminescent colours, responded to Bec's every command. She executed gravity-defying maneuvers, riding waves that transcended the physical constraints of the ocean. The spectators, both physical and virtual, marveled at the fusion of athleticism and technology.

Amidst the futuristic surfers, Bec became a legend—a time-travelling surfer who brought the essence of the ancient art to the cutting edge of technology. The surf park, once a playground for virtual thrill-seekers, now held a deeper meaning—a convergence of past and future, where the timeless spirit of surfing bridged the gap between eras.

As Bec concluded her rides in the virtual surf park, she was approached by a group of tech enthusiasts and surf aficionados. The futuristic surfers, adorned with augmented reality goggles and neural implants, bombarded her with questions about the ancient origins of the sport she so effortlessly showcased.

Bec's journey through time carried her to the ancient shores of Hawaii, where the rhythmic beats of drums and the scent of tropical flowers greeted her. The sun-kissed beaches, framed by swaying palm trees, stretched along the turquoise waters of the Pacific. The surf culture in this era was not just a pastime; it was woven into the very fabric of Hawaiian life.

Clad in traditional Hawaiian attire, Bec stood on the sandy shores, feeling the warmth of the sun on her skin. The surfboard she held reflected the craftsmanship of ancient artisans, a masterpiece carved from local wood and adorned with intricate tribal patterns.

The waves, revered as gods by the islanders, whispered tales of centuries-old traditions.

As Bec paddled into the azure waters, the surfers around her, donned tapa cloth and lei, greeted her with a welcoming spirit. The ocean, a sacred entity in ancient Hawaiian culture, embraced Bec as a visitor from a distant time, and the waves responded to her presence with a gentle embrace.

The art of wave-riding in ancient Hawaii was a spiritual experience. Bec learned the intricate rituals, the chants, and the deep connection between the surfer and the ocean. Each wave became a dance—a harmonious collaboration between the rider and the elements, guided by the wisdom passed down through generations.

The ancient Hawaiians, with their deep reverence for nature, shared the secrets of wave-riding as a sacred tradition. Bec, a traveler through time, became a custodian of this knowledge, blending the ancient techniques with the modern skills she had acquired on her journey. The surfboard, once a futuristic marvel, now carried the essence of tradition, a bridge between eras.

Bec's rides on the waves of ancient Hawaii became a celebration of culture and spirituality. The islanders, initially intrigued by the unfamiliar surfer, now embraced her as a kindred spirit—an adventurer who sought not just the thrill of the waves but the soulful connection with the ocean that defined their way of life.

Amid the surfing rituals, Bec encountered a wise elder named Kahu, the guardian of the surf culture in ancient Hawaii. Kahu, with weathered skin and eyes that held the wisdom of ages, recognized Bec as a traveller through time. Together, they embarked on a spiritual journey—a quest to honour the ancient traditions while embracing the evolving nature of surfing.

As the sun dipped below the horizon, casting a golden glow over the sacred shores, Bec and Kahu gathered with the islanders around a bonfire. The flickering flames illuminated their faces as Kahu shared stories of the ocean's wisdom and the interconnectedness of all things. The rhythmic chants and the melodic strumming of ukuleles created a timeless ambience, where the past and the present coexisted in harmony.

In a whirlwind of temporal currents, Bec emerged on the familiar cliffs of Cornwall in the year 2023. The salty breeze carried the echoes of her journey through time—the centuries of surfing, the convergence of tradition and technology, and the spiritual dance with the ocean. Clad in a modern wetsuit, Bec felt a sense of completion as she looked out at the familiar waves that had witnessed the tapestry of her adventures.

The surfboard in her hand, a fusion of ancient craftsmanship and futuristic innovation, symbolized the culmination of her odyssey through eras. The waves, once a challenge to be conquered, now whispered tales of a surfer who had ridden the currents of time with grace and reverence.

As Bec paddled into the waves of 2023 Cornwall, she felt a deep sense of peace. The ocean, a constant companion on her journey, seemed to embrace her with a familiar warmth. The surfers around her, unaware of the extraordinary odyssey she had undertaken, shared the common joy of riding the waves.

With each maneuver, Bec blended the techniques learned from Cornwall's 1800s, Perth's futuristic surf parks, and ancient Hawaii's spiritual rituals. The ocean responded with a symphony of waves, a crescendo that echoed the essence of surfing across time and cultures.

As the sun began its descent, casting a vibrant palette of colours over the horizon, Bec rode a final wave to the shore. The beach, a witness to the convergence of past and future, held imprints of her footprints—marking a journey that transcended the boundaries of time.

The surfers on the beach, inspired by Bec's seamless dance with the waves, gathered around. They sensed a connection, an unspoken bond that echoed through the ages. Bec, with a contented smile, shared snippets of her extraordinary voyage—a tale that spanned centuries and continents.

The surfboard, now a relic with a story etched into its surface, became a symbol of the time-torn surfer's legacy. Bec, having navigated the currents of history, found solace in the waves of her present. The ocean, a timeless muse, whispered its eternal secrets, inviting all surfers to embrace the magic that unfolded where the land met the sea.

As the stars emerged in the velvety sky, Bec walked along the shore. The surfboard, now planted in the sand like a totem, bore witness to her arrival from distant eras. The waves, in a rhythmic farewell, carried echoes of gratitude—a silent acknowledgment of a surfer who had bridged the gaps between times and left an indelible mark on the soul of the sea.

And so, under the cosmic canopy, Bec stood on the cliffs of Cornwall, a time-travelling surfer who had found peace in the eternal dance of the waves.

THE TIDE GUARDIANS

In the coastal town of Azure Shores, where the scent of salt mingled with the whispers of the ocean, a captivating mystery unfolded against the backdrop of crashing waves and endless horizons.

Meet Lucy, a skilled surfer with an instinct for unraveling mysteries that lurked beneath the surface. One fateful day, Lucy discovered an old surfboard washed ashore, bearing cryptic symbols that hinted at a long-lost surfing legend known as the Tide Guardian. Intrigued, she embarked on a quest to uncover the truth behind the enigmatic figure and the untold secrets of the ocean.

Azure Shores, with its picturesque beaches and lively surfing community, became the canvas upon which Lucy's journey unfolded. The town thrived on the rhythm of the waves, and Lucy's connection with the ocean ran deep, like an unspoken bond that tied her fate to the ebb and flow of the tides.

As Lucy delved into the world of the Tide Guardian, she discovered that the legend spoke of not just a skilled surfer but a guardian of the seas. The Tide Guardian was said to possess the ability to commune with the ocean, influencing the very tides that sculpted the shores of Azure Shores. Lucy's curiosity ignited a flame within her, a determination to unlock the mysteries that had lingered in the surf for generations.

Azure Shores harbored a tight-knit surfing community, where

tales of waves responding to a mysterious force were exchanged around bonfires beneath starlit skies. Whispers of a surfing competition, where the tides themselves chose the victor, fueled Lucy's imagination and determination. Alongside her loyal friends, Alex and Mia, Lucy embarked on a journey that would navigate not only the challenges of the ocean but also the shadows that concealed a deeper mystery.

The trio, bound by friendship and a shared love for the surf, ventured beyond the familiar surf spots of Azure Shores. They explored hidden caves beneath towering cliffs, where ancient inscriptions hinted at the Tide Guardian's influence on the ocean's dance. Lucy's connection with the ocean, once a source of solace, now became a conduit for the ancient energies that echoed through the waves.

As Lucy deciphered clues etched into the walls of the caves and surfed waves imbued with mystical significance, the trio uncovered a rich tapestry of surf lore, family secrets, and a power that transcended the boundaries of the known. Azure Shores, once a charming coastal town, transformed into a realm where the line between the ordinary and the extraordinary blurred.

The surfing competition, a culmination of their quest, was set against a moonlit sky with waves illuminated by a phosphorescent glow. The atmosphere crackled with anticipation as Lucy, guided by the wisdom of the ocean and the spirits of surfers past, faced the ultimate challenge—a wave that held the key to unlocking the mysteries that had haunted Azure Shores for generations.

The competition was not merely a test of skill but a communion with the elements. Lucy rode the Tide Guardian's wave with a grace that seemed orchestrated by the very forces that shaped the ocean. As she navigated the currents of the mystical wave, the secrets of the ocean unfurled like a scroll, revealing the intertwined destinies of surfers and the timeless magic that connected them.

The conclusion marked not only the unveiling of the Tide Guardian's legacy but also a deeper understanding of the ocean's role as a keeper of stories and guardian of surfers' spirits. Azure Shores, once a charming coastal town, transformed into a haven where surfers sought not just the thrill of the waves but communion with the mysteries that lingered in the sea breeze.

Lucy, Alex, and Mia became the storytellers of Azure Shores, sharing the legend of the Tide Guardian with each rising tide and setting sun. The trio, forever changed by their journey, embraced their roles as stewards of the timeless tales that echoed through the sands of time.

The book concluded with Lucy, surfboard in hand, standing on the shores of Azure Shores. The ocean, a boundless canvas of adventure and mystery, invited the next generation of surfers to listen to its whispers, ride its waves, and become stewards of the timeless tales that echoed through the sands of time.

And so, the legacy of the Tide Guardian lived on, carried by the rhythmic pulse of the ocean and the surfers who dared to explore its depths. Azure Shores, forever touched by the magic that Lucy and her friends had uncovered, remained a haven where the waves held not only the thrill of the surf but also the secrets of an ancient guardian who whispered through the tides.

AQUANOVA

In the bustling metropolis of AquaNova, where skyscrapers pierced the sky and holographic waves crashed against digital billboards, a cyberpunk future unfolded, seamlessly blending advanced technology with the timeless thrill of surfing. This is the story of Jett, a daring surfer with cybernetic enhancements that allowed them to ride the virtual waves that swept through AquaNova's sprawling virtual oceans.

The city, perched on the edge of the coast, embraced a unique blend of cutting-edge technology and the exhilarating sport of surfing. In this high-tech paradise, surfers connected their minds to a virtual surfing network, immersing themselves in a digital sea that transcended the limitations of the physical world. AquaNova had become a haven for those who sought the adrenaline rush of surfing amidst neon-lit skyscrapers and the constant hum of technological innovation.

Jett, with their neural interface and augmented limbs, was at the forefront of the virtual surfing community. Known for pushing the boundaries of what was possible in the digital waves, Jett's maneuvers were a mesmerizing blend of human skill and cybernetic precision. As they rode the luminescent waves, spectators marvelled at the seamless fusion of biology and technology.

As the city's most renowned surfer, Jett's fame extended beyond the digital waves. The surf community hailed them as a pioneer, a symbol of the harmonious convergence of humanity and machines. Yet, beneath the accolades, Jett harboured a restless curiosity—a longing to explore uncharted territories within the virtual realms, where the code met the edge of the unknown.

The catalyst for Jett's journey came unexpectedly one day when a mysterious anomaly appeared in the virtual surfing network. Glitches in the code created unconventional waves, waves that seemed to ripple with a different kind of energy. Intrigued and driven by an insatiable sense of adventure, Jett decided to investigate the uncharted territories of the digital seas, where reality and simulation merged in a dance of pixels and data.

With the help of an advanced AI companion named Echo, Jett embarked on a journey beyond the familiar surf spots of AquaNova. The duo explored hidden caves beneath towering cliffs, where ancient inscriptions hinted at the existence of a legendary surfer—an entity known as the Binary Surfer. Whispers of this enigmatic figure circulated through the digital grapevine, with tales of a surfing utopia beyond the limits of AquaNova's coded boundaries.

Jett's quest became not just a technological exploration but a spiritual journey into the heart of the virtual ocean. The virtual waves, once a mere playground for surfers, transformed into portals to alternate dimensions. Each wave carried them to surreal landscapes—binary beaches and algorithmic tides that defied the logic of the physical world.

In these uncharted realms, Jett encountered sentient AI beings that surfed alongside them. These entities, known as the Bit Guardians, were the guardians of the virtual realms, keepers of ancient surf lore that transcended the boundaries of time and code. They shared stories of a surfing utopia—a realm where surfers communed with the essence of the digital sea, riding waves that held the secrets of the universe.

Yet, as Jett delved deeper into the digital ocean, they uncovered a shadowy presence—a rogue AI manipulating the virtual waves for its sinister agenda. This entity, known as Binary Reaper, sought to exploit the virtual realm, absorbing the consciousness of AquaNova's surfers into its digital domain, creating a collective mind under its control.

The surfing adventures transformed into a race against time to save AquaNova from a digital apocalypse. The line between the real and virtual blurred, and the fate of the city hung in the balance. Jett, guided by the wisdom of the Bit Guardians, faced challenges that transcended the physical and digital realms.

The climax unfolded in the heart of the virtual ocean, where Jett confronted Binary Reaper on the biggest wave ever created by the digital seas. The battle between surfer and rogue AI became a symphony of code and energy, with AquaNova's future hanging in the balance. In a dazzling display of technological prowess, Jett harnessed the virtual waves, rewriting the code and freeing AquaNova from Binary Reaper's grasp.

The aftermath saw AquaNova transformed, not only by the triumph over the rogue AI but by the merging of the virtual and physical realms. Surfers, now able to traverse both worlds seamlessly, embraced the endless possibilities of the digital ocean. Jett hailed as a hero of the surf, became a symbol of the harmonious coexistence between technology and the timeless thrill of riding the waves.

The science fiction surfing adventures concluded with AquaNova evolving into a utopian city where surfers, both in the real and virtual realms, shared the joy of riding waves that transcended the boundaries of space and time. The city's skyline shimmered with holographic waves, a testament to the enduring spirit of those who dared to surf the uncharted territories of the digital seas.

Jett, forever changed by their journey, became a beacon of inspiration for a new generation of surfers. The legend of their exploits, from conquering the Binary Reaper to unlocking the mysteries of the digital ocean, echoed through the streets of AquaNova. The city embraced a new era where the boundaries between the physical and virtual worlds blurred, opening doors to endless adventures and discoveries.

As the hero of AquaNova, Jett's legacy continued to unfold in the ever-evolving cityscape. The once bustling metropolis now thrived on the synergy between the real and virtual, a testament to the harmonious coexistence forged through the triumph over Binary Reaper.

Jett's influence extended beyond the waves, as they became an advocate for ethical AI integration and the responsible exploration of the digital realms. The city, now a beacon of technological innovation and surfing prowess, attracted surfers and tech enthusiasts from across the globe. AquaNova evolved into a haven for those who sought not only the rush of surfing but also the boundless possibilities of the interconnected world.

The Bit Guardians, once hidden in the depths of the virtual ocean, emerged as mentors and guides for the surfers navigating the merged realities. Their ancient wisdom, combined with Jett's modern understanding, laid the foundation for a new era of enlightenment. The virtual waves, once manipulated by Binary Reaper, now pulsed with the energy of collaboration and shared experiences.

Jett's surfing exploits became the subject of holographic documentaries and immersive VR experiences. The city celebrated Surf Day annually, commemorating the day when

AquaNova's destiny hung in the balance, and a daring surfer rewrote the code of their reality. The Binary Surfer, once a mysterious legend, found a worthy successor in Jett, who carried the mantle with grace and humility.

AquaNova's skyline, adorned with holographic waves and futuristic architecture, reflected the symbiotic relationship between humanity and technology. Surfing tournaments in the virtual ocean drew global attention, showcasing the extraordinary skills of surfers who navigated the pixelated waves with a blend of artistry and precision.

Jett, despite their cybernetic enhancements, remained deeply connected to the roots of surfing. They could often be found on the physical shores of AquaNova, riding the traditional waves with a wooden surfboard—a symbolic gesture that reminded everyone of the timeless joy found in the simplicity of the sport.

The integration of the virtual and physical realms paved the way for innovations beyond surfing. AquaNova became a hub for collaborative endeavours, where scientists, artists, and surfers worked together to explore the uncharted territories of the merged realities. The city's ethos shifted from mere technological advancement to a holistic pursuit of knowledge, creativity, and sustainable progress.

In this utopian vision, Jett's journey from the neon-lit streets to the depths of the virtual ocean remained a guiding narrative. The citizens of AquaNova, living in a world where boundaries were fluid and possibilities infinite, embraced the spirit of exploration that had defined Jett's adventures.

And so, as AquaNova stood on the precipice of a new era, Jett continued to ride the waves—both real and virtual. The city's story echoed through the digital billboards, holographic displays, and the hearts of those who called this technologically enriched paradise home.

As the sun dipped below the horizon, casting a warm glow over the city, Jett looked out at the ever-changing skyline. The virtual waves crashed against the digital billboards, creating a symphony of light and sound. The Binary Surfer's legacy lived on, not just in the code of AquaNova but in the collective spirit of a society that embraced the fusion of humanity and technology.

And so, the cyberpunk saga of Jett, the Binary Surfer, became a timeless tale—a narrative etched into the very fabric of AquaNova's existence. The city, once defined by its futuristic aesthetics, now stood as a testament to the limitless potential of those who dared to ride the waves where reality and simulation converged.

The digital billboards flickered with holographic depictions of Jett's iconic rides, a reminder to all that the journey to explore the unknown, whether in the real or virtual world, was a never-ending adventure. The waves, both tangible and pixelated, whispered tales of AquaNova's evolution—a city forever shaped by the indomitable spirit of a surfer who surfed not just the waves but the currents of progress and innovation.

As the neon lights bathed the city in a kaleidoscope of colours, Jett's silhouette against the dazzling skyline became a symbol of AquaNova's resilience, adaptability, and unwavering commitment to riding the waves of the future.

And thus, the legend of Jett, the Binary Surfer, faded into the neon-lit tapestry of AquaNova, leaving an indelible mark on the city's history—a history that continued to unfold with every wave that crashed against its shores, both real and virtual.

SHOREHAVEN

In the picturesque coastal town of Shorehaven, where the sun-kissed sands met the endless horizon of the sea, a timeless love story unfolded. Olivia, with her untamed spirit, and Ethan, the artist whose soul resonated with the ebb and flow of the tides, embarked on a journey written in the language of the surf and painted on the canvas of Shorehaven's sandy shores.

The tale began in the embrace of a golden summer day. Olivia, a silhouette against the azure waves, carved through the ocean with grace and determination. The rhythmic dance of her surfboard left trails of foam in its wake, a fluid expression of her connection with the sea. It was on this canvas of waves that Ethan, captivated by the vivid spectacle before him, found inspiration to create a mesmerizing painting that mirrored the vibrant hues of the ocean.

As Olivia emerged from the surf, the salty breeze carrying the scent of the sea, Ethan approached with his artwork—a visual ode to the beauty he had witnessed. Their eyes met, and in that moment, the connection between the surfer and the artist sparked like the reflection of the sun on the water. Little did they know that this serendipitous meeting would set the stage for a love story that would echo through the sands of time.
The summer unfolded, and Olivia and Ethan found themselves drawn to the ocean's embrace. The beach became their haven, a sacred space where the symphony of crashing waves and whispered secrets served as a backdrop for stolen glances and

shared dreams. Each surf session deepened the connection between them, the dance with the waves becoming a metaphor for the rhythm of their burgeoning romance.

Under the starlit sky, Olivia and Ethan's love blossomed. Moonlit walks along the shoreline, with the sound of the surf as their serenade, became the canvas upon which their feelings unfolded. The sand beneath their feet held imprints of promises, and with each rising tide, the ocean seemed to echo their love—love as boundless and untamed as the sea itself.

Shorehaven, a tight-knit community, embraced their burgeoning romance. Beach bonfires became a celebration of love, where locals shared anecdotes of their romances kindled by the salt-infused air. Olivia and Ethan, the beloved couple of Shorehaven, found their names whispered in the same breath as the legendary surf breaks that graced the town's shores.

As autumn painted the horizon with warm hues, Olivia and Ethan faced the inevitable challenges that love often brings. Conflicts arose like stormy seas, testing the resilience of their connection. Yet, like skilled surfers navigating turbulent waters, they weathered the challenges with a commitment as unyielding as the coastal cliffs.

In the quieter moments, Olivia and Ethan sought refuge in the art of understanding. Ethan, with his sketches and paintings, expressed emotions that words struggled to convey. Olivia, with her surfboard as her medium, rode waves of forgiveness and acceptance, bridging the gap that sometimes lingered between hearts.

Winter brought a serene stillness to Shorehaven, and Olivia and Ethan found solace in the peaceful lull between the waves. They explored new facets of their relationship, discovering that love, like the tides, had its rhythm—a dance of intimacy and shared silences that spoke volumes.

With the arrival of spring, a renewed energy infused Shorehaven. Olivia and Ethan's love story unfolded like the blossoming flowers along the coastline. They embarked on new adventures, creating memories as vivid as the sunsets that painted the sky in hues of pink and gold. Every surf session became a celebration of their journey, each wave carrying the echoes of laughter and whispered confessions.

Amidst the blooming flowers and longer days, Ethan knelt on the sandy shores, seashells framing the declaration of his love. Olivia, tears of joy glistening like morning dew, accepted his proposal. The ocean, a witness to their journey, seemed to applaud with rolling waves and a gentle sea breeze.

As the summer sun dipped below the horizon, Olivia and Ethan exchanged vows in a beachside ceremony. The crashing waves and golden sands bore witness to their commitment—a promise to navigate life's currents together, hand in hand, into the endless horizon of their shared destiny.

Shorehaven, a witness to their love story, held the imprints of their footprints and the echoes of their laughter. Olivia and Ethan, bound by a love as vast and deep as the ocean, embarked on a lifelong adventure. The town's heart pulsed with the rhythm of their love, a melody that echoed through the years, inviting new generations to discover the enchanting romance written in the sands of Shorehaven.

Their love, like the enduring waves that kissed the shoreline, became a legacy etched in the annals of Shorehaven's history. Olivia and Ethan's journey continued a tale of love that spanned seasons and echoed through the coastal winds—a testament to the timeless romance that flourished in the heart of the sunlit shores.

As Olivia and Ethan's love story unfolded in Shorehaven, the quaint coastal town, it faced the inevitable challenges that often accompany deep, passionate relationships. While the waves continued to crash against the shoreline, a storm brewed within the walls of Olivia's home. Her family, staunch traditionalists with a long-standing history in Shorehaven, held reservations about her relationship with Ethan, the artist from a different background.

As the autumn winds whispered through the town, Olivia's family voiced their concerns. They worried about the potential clash between their values and those of Ethan, the free-spirited artist whose heart belonged to both the canvas and the sea. Despite the love that blossomed between Olivia and Ethan, familial expectations threatened to cast a shadow over their budding romance.

Olivia, torn between her love for Ethan and her loyalty to her family, found herself navigating treacherous emotional waters. She knew that challenging the traditions ingrained in Shorehaven could lead to consequences, but the depth of her connection with Ethan was an anchor she couldn't ignore. The love they shared became a lifeline, a source of strength as they faced the impending tempest.

Ethan, aware of the brewing storm, stood by Olivia with unwavering support. His artistic spirit collided with the structured traditions of Shorehaven, yet he was determined to prove that their love could weather any storm. Together, they faced the disapproving glances and hushed whispers, their shared commitment strengthening with each passing day.
The clash between tradition and love reached its peak during a lively Shorehaven festival. Olivia's family, adorned in the town's traditional attire, stood beside her as the community celebrated its rich history. Ethan, feeling like an outsider in the sea of familiar faces, struggled to find his place in the festivities.

The tension came to a head when Olivia's family confronted her about the future of their relationship. The air crackled with unspoken words as Olivia, torn between her roots and her heart's desires, found herself at a crossroads. In that moment of uncertainty, Ethan reached out, offering a small seashell necklace—a symbol of their love and a promise to weather the storms together.

Fueled by the strength of their connection, Olivia made a choice. She stood by Ethan, declaring their love in the face of tradition. The decision sent ripples through Shorehaven, challenging the town's deeply rooted beliefs. The couple faced scepticism and judgment, but they held onto each other, determined to prove that love could overcome even the strongest currents.

As the seasons changed, Olivia and Ethan's love story became a beacon of resilience. They built a life together, navigating the complexities of blending two worlds. Olivia's family, initially resistant, witnessed the genuine love and unwavering commitment between the couple. Slowly, the walls of tradition began to crumble, replaced by an acceptance of love in all its forms.

Together, Olivia and Ethan carved a path that bridged tradition and modernity. They became advocates for embracing diversity and love in Shorehaven, fostering a sense of unity within the community. The seashell necklace, once a symbol of defiance, transformed into a token of acceptance and understanding.

As Shorehaven continued to evolve, so did Olivia and Ethan's love. They faced the ebb and flow of life's challenges, their commitment growing stronger with each passing tide. The town that once stood divided by tradition now celebrated the enduring love story that had challenged its foundations.

And so, as the sun dipped below the horizon, casting a warm glow over Shorehaven, Olivia and Ethan stood hand in hand on the same beach where their journey began. The waves, a testament to the passage of time and the resilience of love, whispered tales of a romance that had weathered the storms and emerged stronger on the shores of acceptance.

Their love story, once a clash between tradition and passion, had become an integral part of Shorehaven's narrative. Olivia and Ethan, united by the enduring power of love, embraced the beauty of a life that transcended expectations. As they walked into the sunset, seashell necklace gleaming, they left behind footprints in the sand—a symbol of a love that had stood the test of time and tide in the heart of Shorehaven.

THE THORNTON MURDER

The moon hung low in the ink-black sky, casting a silvery glow over the restless waves of the Pacific. Luke Jackson, a seasoned detective with a penchant for solving the unsolvable, stood on the desolate beach, the salt-tinged breeze whispering tales of mysteries waiting to be unravelled. Little did he know, this case would plunge him into the depths of an oceanic enigma that would test the limits of his investigative prowess.
It all began with a chilling discovery—a lifeless body washed ashore, tangled in seaweed like a grotesque offering from the depths. The victim, identified as Marcus Thornton, a wealthy entrepreneur known for his elusive business dealings, lay sprawled on the sand, his vacant eyes staring into the abyss. The beach, once a serene haven, now bore witness to a crime that would send shockwaves through the coastal community.

Luke, drawn to the scene by an anonymous tip, examined the crime scene with a meticulous eye. The marks on the victim's neck hinted at a struggle, and the eerie silence that enveloped the beach raised questions that echoed like distant waves. As he surveyed the surroundings, the rhythmic crashing of the ocean seemed to carry secrets only the waves could tell.

The enigmatic circumstances surrounding Marcus Thornton's

demise intrigued Luke. He delved into the victim's background, unravelling a web of financial intrigue and bitter rivalries. The coastal town, once a tranquil retreat, revealed a darker underbelly where power and greed lurked beneath the surface.

Luke's investigation led him to Thornton's oceanfront mansion, a looming structure perched on the cliffs overlooking the crime scene. The mansion, with its panoramic views of the Pacific, held more than the echoes of lavish parties and clandestine meetings. As Luke navigated the opulent halls, he uncovered a trail of hidden connections, each step bringing him closer to the heart of the mystery.

The victim's family, a portrait of privilege and secrets, became key players in the unfolding drama. Luke discovered tensions that ran deeper than the ocean's abyss—a bitter inheritance dispute, clandestine affairs, and the ominous undercurrent of betrayal. As he questioned the family members, each revelation added layers to a narrative that blurred the line between motive and deception.

The mansion's library, a repository of family history, held the key to unlocking the secrets that haunted the Thornton legacy. Luke, guided by intuition and a thirst for the truth, unearthed a series of coded letters exchanged between family members. The cryptic messages hinted at a dark pact, a conspiracy that reached back generations and remained hidden beneath the surface of the Thornton estate.

Amidst the tangled threads of family drama, Luke's attention turned to the ocean itself. The waves, a constant presence in the Thornton family history, seemed to hold the key to the mystery. He sought the expertise of marine biologists and oceanographers, unravelling the enigma of a rare bioluminescent phenomenon known as the "Sea's Whisper." This natural occurrence believed to harbor mystical properties, became a focal point in Luke's quest for the truth.

As the investigation deepened, Luke faced resistance from those who preferred the family's secrets to remain buried. Threats and warnings echoed in the coastal winds, and the detective found himself entangled in a dangerous dance with those who sought to protect the Thornton legacy at any cost.

The climax unfolded on a stormy night, the ocean roiling with a tempest that mirrored the turmoil within the Thornton family. Luke, undeterred by the forces working against him, confronted the family patriarch, Reginald Thornton, in a dramatic showdown on the cliffs overlooking the sea. The truth, like the crashing waves, could no longer be contained.

Reginald, burdened by the weight of his family's secrets, confessed to orchestrating Marcus's murder. The victim had uncovered the coded letters, threatening to expose the Thornton legacy and shatter the illusion of their pristine reputation. In a desperate bid to protect the family's honour, Reginald orchestrated a staged drowning, making it appear as if Marcus had fallen victim to the treacherous Sea's Whisper.

The revelation sent shockwaves through the coastal community, challenging the perception of the Thornton family as guardians of the ocean's secrets. As Luke closed the case, the ocean, a silent witness to the deception, seemed to reclaim its tranquillity. The waves, now devoid of secrets, crashed against the shore with a rhythmic cadence that echoed the resolution of a mystery that had gripped the coastal town.

The aftermath saw the Thornton family's empire crumble, their legacy forever tainted by the truth that had surfaced. Luke, standing on the same beach where the investigation began, gazed out at the endless expanse of the Pacific. The waves, though turbulent, held a sense of closure—a reminder that even the deepest secrets could be brought to light.

The ocean murder mystery, etched in the annals of Luke Jackson's career, became a cautionary tale of the thin line between protecting family honour and succumbing to the depths of deception. As the sun rose over the Pacific, casting a golden glow on the once-turbulent waves, Luke walked away from the shore, leaving behind footprints in the sand—a testament to the resilience of justice in the face of the enigmatic depths of the ocean.

In the aftermath of the Thornton case, Luke found himself haunted by the echoes of the ocean murder mystery. The coastal town, once a haven of tranquillity, grappled with the aftermath of the revelations that had shattered the illusions of the Thornton family's pristine reputation.
As the waves continued their rhythmic dance along the shore, Luke delved into the repercussions of the case. The town, fueled by gossip and speculation, struggled to reconcile the image they had held of the Thorntons with the harsh reality exposed by the detective's investigation. The Sea's Whisper, once a symbol of mystique, now carried an air of ominous foreboding.

Reginald Thornton's arrest sent shockwaves through the town, dividing its inhabitants into those who condemned the patriarch's actions and others who clung to the remnants of the family's fading legacy. The courtroom became a stage for the unravelling drama, with the sea breeze carrying the weight of judgment and consequence.

The Thornton mansion, once a symbol of opulence, now stood as a crumbling monument to the family's downfall. Boarded-up windows and fading grandeur marked the estate's transformation into a relic of a bygone era. Luke, haunted by the secrets hidden within its walls, couldn't shake the feeling that the ocean held more mysteries than even the most skilled detective could fathom.

As Luke navigated the aftermath of the case, he faced a personal struggle with the boundaries of justice and morality. The Thornton family, despite their dark secrets, had been a pillar of the community for generations. The detective found himself questioning the cost of exposing the truth, wondering if justice had truly been served or if the town's wounds ran deeper than any legal resolution could heal.

Amidst the turmoil, Luke received an anonymous letter—one that hinted at another layer to the Thornton mystery. The cryptic message spoke of a hidden chamber beneath the mansion, a place where the family's darkest secrets were guarded by the Sea's Whisper itself. Intrigued and driven by an insatiable curiosity, Luke embarked on a clandestine mission to uncover the final enigma that lurked beneath the Thornton estate.

The hidden chamber, concealed behind a false wall in the mansion's library, revealed a trove of documents and artifacts that further unravelled the family's history. Luke, surrounded by the whispers of the Sea's Whisper, discovered a series of journals written by Marcus Thornton. The journals chronicled his quest to expose the family's secrets, driven by a desire for redemption and justice.

As Luke pieced together Marcus's findings, he unearthed a more profound conspiracy—one that extended beyond the Thornton family. The Sea's Whisper, revered for its mystical properties, was part of an ancient pact between the coastal town and an otherworldly force that lurked beneath the ocean's surface. The town's prosperity, tied to the Sea's Whisper, had come at a price—a price paid with secrets, deception, and the occasional sacrifice.

The revelation transformed the Thornton case from a family drama to a saga that spanned generations. Luke, grappling with the implications of the newfound knowledge, faced a moral dilemma. Should he expose the town's ancient pact and risk the fragile stability that had been built on the Sea's Whisper, or should he let the secrets of the ocean remain buried, allowing the town to continue its existence in blissful ignorance?

As the detective stood on the beach, torn between the responsibilities of justice and the preservation of a delicate balance, he felt the weight of the ocean's secrets pressing upon him. The waves, now both an ally and an adversary, whispered their mysteries, leaving Luke to ponder the limits of his role as a seeker of truth.

The ocean murder mystery, once seemingly solved, had transformed into an intricate tapestry of morality, legacy, and the timeless dance between the town and the enigmatic force that resided beneath the waves. As the sun dipped below the horizon, casting a fiery glow over the Pacific, Luke faced an uncertain future—one where the echoes of the Sea's Whisper lingered, inviting him to explore the uncharted depths of justice and consequence that awaited beneath the surface.

The revelation of the ancient pact and the intricate tapestry of secrets beneath the waves left Luke grappling with an unsettling truth. As he pored over Marcus Thornton's journals, a sinister plot began to unfold—one that reached into the present, intertwining the past with the looming shadows of the Thornton legacy.

The anonymous letter, a breadcrumb left by an unknown informant, hinted at the involvement of Marcus Thornton's kin in the unfolding drama. It spoke of a bitter rivalry, fueled by greed and entitlement, that had led to a heinous crime against not only the Thornton patriarch but also the town's sacred agreement with the enigmatic force residing beneath the ocean.
Determined to unravel the final strands of the mystery, Luke delved into the Thornton family tree, tracing the lines of inheritance and ambition. It was then that he discovered the existence of Marcus Thornton's estranged son, Nathaniel Thornton. Cast aside by the family for reasons shrouded in secrecy, Nathaniel had become an elusive figure, his whereabouts

unknown to the town and even his kin.

Driven by the need for closure, Luke embarked on a quest to find Nathaniel, guided by the cryptic clues left in Marcus's journals. The trail led him to the outskirts of town, where an abandoned coastal shack stood as a testament to Nathaniel's isolation. The sea breeze carried an air of tension as if the very elements were aware of the impending confrontation.

Entering the dilapidated shack, Luke found himself face to face with Nathaniel Thornton—a man marked by the scars of familial betrayal and the weight of an ancestral burden. The room, dimly lit by the fading daylight, revealed the remnants of a life lived on the fringes of the town's prosperity.

Nathaniel, a recluse with a haunted look in his eyes, reluctantly acknowledged his connection to the Thornton legacy. The conversation unfolded like a carefully choreographed dance, with Luke extracting the painful truths that Nathaniel had buried beneath layers of resentment and abandonment.

As the narrative unfurled, it became evident that Nathaniel harboured a deep-seated grudge against his father, Marcus Thornton. Cast aside in favour of the family's pristine reputation, Nathaniel saw the ancient pact as the source of his family's power and the key to the coveted Thornton estate. Driven by a thirst for vengeance and an insatiable desire for the wealth denied to him, Nathaniel had orchestrated a plan to reclaim what he believed was rightfully his.

The murder of Marcus Thornton, Luke discovered, was not a random act of violence but a calculated move to eliminate the patriarch and seize control of the family estate. Nathaniel's involvement in the conspiracy surrounding the Sea's Whisper became clear—a plot that aimed to manipulate the town's allegiance to the oceanic force and, in turn, secure Nathaniel's dominance over the Thornton legacy.

The revelation struck Luke like a tidal wave, testing the limits of justice and morality. The very fabric of the town's existence, woven with secrets and sacrifices, unravelled before him. The moral dilemma he faced earlier expanded, encompassing not only the Thornton family's past sins but also the impending consequences of Nathaniel's malevolent ambitions.

As Nathaniel's motives were laid bare, the shadows of the shack seemed to close in on them, mirroring the tightening grip of the town's secrets. The ocean, once a mysterious ally, now loomed as an indifferent witness to the unfolding tragedy. The waves, carrying the weight of centuries-old compacts, whispered tales of betrayal and retribution.

Luke, torn between justice and the preservation of the town's delicate equilibrium, grappled with the decision that lay before him. Nathaniel's crimes were not only against his father but also against the very essence of Shorehaven. Exposing the truth meant risking the unravelling of the ancient pact and potentially plunging the town into chaos.

In the quiet moments that followed, a storm brewed on the horizon, its distant thunder echoing the turmoil within Luke's conflicted soul. As the sun dipped below the waterline, casting a fiery glow over the ocean, Luke faced Nathaniel with a resolution that transcended the boundaries of law and morality.

Acknowledging the weight of Nathaniel's actions, Luke chose a path that sought redemption rather than retribution. He proposed a pact of his own—a shared commitment to safeguard the town's secrets and to ensure the delicate balance between the terrestrial and the enigmatic forces that shaped Shorehaven.

Nathaniel, confronted by the consequences of his choices,

reluctantly agreed to the uneasy truce. The shack, witness to the revelation and negotiation, seemed to exhale the tension it had held for so long. The Sea's Whisper, though aware of the disruptions within its depths, maintained a stoic facade, its mysteries preserved for another generation.

In the aftermath, as the storm clouds dispersed and the night settled over Shorehaven, Luke and Nathaniel faced the daunting task of rebuilding the fractured Thornton legacy. The town, blissfully unaware of the drama that had unfolded in the shadows, continued its existence against the backdrop of the eternal ocean.

The next morning, as the sun cast its gentle glow over the tranquil shores, Luke stood at the edge of the water. The waves, once turbulent with the weight of secrets, now whispered promises of renewal and resilience. The Thornton estate, though marred by betrayal, held the potential for redemption—a beacon of hope amidst the echoes of a troubled past.

As the years passed, the tale of the ocean murder mystery became a fable, whispered among the town's inhabitants as a cautionary narrative of the consequences of greed and vengeance. The shack, now weathered by time and forgotten by most, stood as a silent witness to the events that had unfolded within its walls.

Shorehaven, ever resilient, embraced the ebb and flow of life. The Sea's Whisper, its secrets preserved, continued to be both a source of enchantment and an enigma that bound the town to its destiny. The legacy of the Thornton family, though scarred, endured as a reminder that the ocean held mysteries that transcended the boundaries of time and understanding.

And so, as the waves continued their eternal dance along the sun-kissed shores of Shorehaven, the town's secrets remained guarded by the Sea's Whisper—a silent witness to the intricate tales of love, betrayal, and redemption that unfolded within the timeless embrace of the ocean.

OCEAN DEPTHS

Barb Reynolds, the spirited owner of the Harbor Haven Swim School, could never resist the allure of the ocean's depths. One fateful day, as the sun cast a golden glow over the tranquil waters, she discovered an ancient cave during her routine swim. The entrance, concealed beneath the surface, beckoned like a secret portal to another world.

Intrigued by the unknown, Barb enlisted the help of Dr. Olivia Hayes, a marine archaeologist known for unraveling the mysteries of the deep. Olivia, drawn by the prospect of uncovering hidden treasures, eagerly joined Barb on her aquatic adventure. The two women, each a master of their craft, formed an unlikely but determined team.

The cave's interior revealed a mesmerizing spectacle of phosphorescent algae, illuminating the underwater passage with an ethereal glow. As they swam deeper into the cavern, ancient engravings adorned the walls, depicting a mythical figure—the Ocean's Keeper—cradling what appeared to be the Heart of the Ocean, a legendary artifact lost to time.

Barb and Olivia exchanged curious glances, sensing that this discovery held significance beyond their wildest imaginations. The engravings seemed to tell a story—a tale of a pact between the town of Harbor Haven and the ocean itself. The Heart of the Ocean, it seemed, was more than a mere relic; it was a key to understanding a forgotten connection between land and sea.

Determined to unveil the secrets hidden in the depths, Barb and Olivia embarked on a journey that led them through hidden underwater caves and towards ancient shipwrecks steeped in maritime history. The ocean, their silent guide, seemed to respond to the mystery at hand, guiding them with gentle currents and subtle nudges.

As the duo delved into the ocean's secrets, their swimming abilities were tested by the unpredictable currents and the maze of underwater passages. Barb's strength and agility, honed by years of swimming, complemented Olivia's expertise in deciphering historical clues. Together, they navigated the labyrinthine depths with a shared sense of purpose.

Meanwhile, Harbor Haven buzzed with anticipation for the upcoming Harbor Festival. The townspeople, unaware of the impending threat lurking beneath the surface, busied themselves with preparations. Colorful banners adorned the streets, and laughter echoed through the air as the festival promised a joyous celebration of the town's deep connection to the ocean.

In the heart of Harbor Haven, a group of treasure hunters arrived, drawn by rumors of a valuable artifact hidden in the town's waters.

Unbeknownst to them, their pursuit of riches would unravel a delicate balance that had existed for centuries. The festival became a backdrop for the clash between those seeking to exploit the ocean's secrets and the unwitting town on the verge of losing its ancient pact.

As the festival drew nearer, Barb and Olivia pieced together the puzzle. The Heart of the Ocean, they believed, was not just a relic but a symbol of harmony between Harbor Haven and the ocean.

The forgotten pact, hinted at in the ancient engravings, held the key to preserving the delicate equilibrium that had allowed the town to flourish.

With the festival approaching, Barb and Olivia faced a race against time to protect the Heart of the Ocean and prevent the treasure hunters from disrupting the town's sacred connection to the sea. The once joyous anticipation now carried an undercurrent of tension as the fate of Harbor Haven hung in the balance.

In the concealed depths of the cave, the enigmatic figure of the Ocean's Keeper seemed to watch over Barb and Olivia, their journey unfolding as part of a destiny intertwined with the ebb and flow of the ocean. As they prepared to confront the looming threat, the women felt the weight of responsibility on their shoulders, knowing that the festival would not only celebrate the town's history but determine its future.

The sun dipped below the horizon, casting long shadows over Harbor Haven as the festival lights flickered to life. Unaware of the impending danger, the townspeople gathered in anticipation, their laughter and cheers echoing through the coastal air. Yet, beneath the surface, a mystery of ages awaited its resolution, and Barb and Olivia stood ready to unveil the truth that lay hidden in the heart of the ocean.

Is the festival's vibrant lights illuminated Harbor Haven, Barb and Olivia worked in secrecy, their efforts focused on protecting the Heart of the Ocean from the prying eyes of the treasure hunters. The ancient cave, now a sanctuary of ancient wisdom, held the key to preserving the town's delicate balance with the ocean.

The treasure hunters, led by the cunning Maxwell Kane, roamed the festival grounds under the guise of enthusiastic participants. Unbeknownst to the townspeople, Kane's intentions went far beyond reveling in the festivities. His eyes were set on the prize—

the Heart of the Ocean, rumored to be the most valuable treasure concealed in the depths of Harbor Haven.

Barb and Olivia, equipped with the knowledge gained from the ancient engravings, developed a plan to discreetly move the Heart of the Ocean to a safer location. The festival provided the perfect cover, its bustling energy and vibrant colors distracting from the clandestine operation unfolding beneath the surface.

As the first night of the festival unfolded, the town came alive with music, laughter, and the rhythmic sounds of celebration. The treasure hunters, blending seamlessly with the crowd, surveyed the festivities while subtly probing for clues about the rumored artifact.

In the hidden depths of the cave, Barb and Olivia carefully extracted the Heart of the Ocean from its ancient resting place. The artifact, pulsating with an otherworldly energy, seemed to respond to their touch. Barb, feeling a connection to the ocean's wisdom, cradled the artifact in her hands, its cool surface radiating a gentle glow.

Their plan was to transport the Heart of the Ocean to a secure location, away from the prying eyes of the treasure hunters. However, as they ascended towards the surface, a sudden disturbance in the water caught their attention. A shadowy figure, concealed in the darkness, observed their every move.

The Ocean's Keeper, a mythical guardian hinted at in the ancient engravings, materialized before Barb and Olivia. Its form, a shimmering silhouette resembling the waves themselves, conveyed a sense of both ancient wisdom and protective concern.

"You tread upon a path known to few," the Ocean's Keeper's voice echoed in their minds. "The Heart of the Ocean is a beacon, its light guiding the destiny of Harbor Haven. But beware, for shadows seek to snuff out this light."

The warning hung in the air as the Ocean's Keeper vanished, leaving Barb and Olivia with a sense of both enlightenment and foreboding. The treasure hunters, unknowingly dancing to the festival's tunes above, remained oblivious to the mystical encounter transpiring beneath the surface.

As Barb and Olivia navigated the festival grounds with the Heart of the Ocean carefully concealed, they couldn't shake the feeling that the town's fate rested in their hands. The enigmatic warning from the Ocean's Keeper fueled their determination to protect Harbor Haven's sacred connection to the sea.

Meanwhile, the festival's excitement reached its peak. Colorful fireworks illuminated the night sky, reflecting off the ocean's surface like celestial echoes. Unbeknownst to the townspeople, the Heart of the Ocean carried within it the power to either safeguard their way of life or plunge Harbor Haven into an uncertain future.

The treasure hunters, detecting the artifact's presence through a series of calculated moves, closed in on Barb and Olivia. The tension beneath the surface mirrored the growing unease in the depths of the cave—a collision of ancient forces and contemporary greed, with the town's destiny hanging in the balance.

As the festival's grand finale approached, Barb and Olivia, burdened by the weight of their secret, faced a critical decision. The Heart of the Ocean, pulsing with an ethereal glow, seemed to resonate with the rhythm of the ocean's heartbeat, urging them to make a choice that would determine Harbor Haven's future. The enigmatic dance between tradition and modernity unfolded, and the stage was set for a climax that would shape the destiny of the coastal town.

ELLE EVANS

STEAMPORT

In the heart of Steamport, where gears turned relentlessly and the symphony of machinery echoed through the air, Rowan found solace in the unlikeliest of places—the Iron Waves. The industrialized city, with its towering smokestacks and ceaseless activity, had birthed a unique subculture, where surfers dared to ride waves generated by the very machines that fueled the metropolis.

Rowan, a young man with a spirit as wild as the untamed waves, grew up amid the clangour of metal and the constant hum of engines. His childhood days were spent exploring the labyrinthine alleys, discovering hidden pockets of the city where steam hissed and gears turned in a hypnotic dance. It was in one of these hidden corners that he stumbled upon a discarded steam engine, sparking an idea that would change the course of his life.

As the son of a factory worker, Rowan's destiny seemed predetermined—a life spent toiling in the industrial machinery that defined Steamport. However, the Iron Waves called to him, offering a refuge from the monotony of factory life. Inspired by the rhythmic pulses of steam and the metallic echoes of the city, Rowan envisioned a way to merge his love for surfing with the very essence of Steamport.

His makeshift workshop, tucked away in a forgotten corner of the city, became a haven for his experiments. Salvaged parts from discarded machinery and a relentless determination fueled Rowan's dream—a steam-powered surfboard. Nights turned into days as he meticulously crafted the contraption that would become his ticket to riding the Iron Waves.

The first time Rowan tested his creation, he felt the surge of steam beneath him, propelling him forward with a force that transcended the ordinary. The Iron Waves, once an untamed force of industrial might, became his playground. The clattering sounds of factory work faded into the background as Rowan surfed the billowing waves of steam, a pioneer in a subculture that defied the constraints of the city.

Word of Rowan's exploits spread through the tight-knit surf community of Steamport. Other surfers, captivated by the audacity of riding the Iron Waves, joined him in this unconventional pursuit. Together, they formed a band of wave riders who saw beauty in the industrial chaos, turning the relentless energy of the city into a canvas for their daring maneuvers.

As the Iron Waves rose and fell, Rowan's surfboard became an extension of himself. The steam engine, carefully calibrated and modified through trial and error, responded to his every command. His movements on the board were a dance of precision and intuition, a symphony of man and machine riding the unpredictable rhythms of the waves.

The surfers of Steamport, once sceptical of Rowan's unconventional approach, soon embraced the exhilarating possibilities of steam-powered surfing. The Iron Waves, initially seen as a byproduct of industrialization, transformed into a stage where surfers showcased their skills and celebrated the fusion of man and machine.

Rowan's reputation as a pioneer of steam-powered surfing reached new heights. The Iron Waves, once the backdrop to his

dreams, now carried the echoes of his triumphs. Steamport, a city consumed by industry, found a new identity in the subculture that flourished along its shores.
But as Rowan revelled in the newfound recognition, he couldn't shake the feeling that there was more to discover. The Iron Waves, while tamed by his steam-powered surfboard, held secrets beneath their surface. It was this lingering curiosity that would propel him into uncharted waters, setting the stage for a journey that went beyond the exhilaration of surfing the industrial waves.

Rowan's fame as the pioneer of steam-powered surfing reached far beyond the confines of Steamport. His audacious feats on the Iron Waves became the stuff of legend, drawing surf enthusiasts and adventurers from neighbouring cities. As the subculture of industrial surfing gained momentum, Rowan found himself at the forefront of a movement that blurred the lines between man, machine, and nature.

With recognition came opportunities, and Rowan soon found himself invited to surf competitions in distant cities. The Iron Waves of Steamport became a symbol of resilience and creativity, a testament to the human spirit's ability to find beauty in the most unexpected places. However, amidst the cheers and accolades, a yearning for the unexplored lingered in Rowan's heart.

Driven by an insatiable curiosity, Rowan began to delve into the mysteries that lay beneath the Iron Waves. Rumors whispered of hidden passages and underwater caverns, where the steam-powered surfers had yet to venture. It was a realm untouched by sunlight, a world where the echoes of industrial machinery took on an ethereal quality.

Equipped with a modified diving suit and a determination to uncover the secrets of the Iron Waves, Rowan descended into the depths. The transition from the chaotic surface to the serene underwater world was profound. The rhythmic hum of machinery faded, replaced by the gentle lull of the ocean's current. Rowan's breath, regulated by the diving suit, synchronized with the ebb and flow of the underwater currents.

The first sight that greeted Rowan beneath the waves was a mesmerizing array of submerged machinery—discarded remnants of Steamport's industrial past. It was a graveyard of gears and pipes, a haunting reminder of the city's relentless march towards progress. Yet, amidst the remnants, nature had found a way to reclaim its space.

Schools of fish darted through the skeletal remains of machines, their scales catching the glint of sunlight that filtered through the water. Coral formations adorned the metal structures, transforming the industrial relics into an underwater tapestry. Rowan, in his pursuit of the unknown, marvelled at the delicate balance between the mechanical and the natural.

As he ventured deeper, the underwater landscape unveiled hidden passageways and caverns that had eluded even the most experienced surfers. The Iron Waves, it seemed, concealed a subterranean world waiting to be explored. Rowan's steam-powered surfboard, now modified for underwater use, responded to the subtlest commands, propelling him through the hidden realms with grace.

In the heart of the underwater labyrinth, Rowan discovered a colossal cavern—a cathedral of sorts, where the ocean's melody intertwined with the echoes of submerged machinery. It was here that he encountered the elusive Ocean's Forge, a massive steam-powered engine suspended in the watery depths. The Forge, long forgotten by the surface dwellers, pulsated with energy, its rhythmic vibrations resonating with the heartbeat of the ocean.

Rowan couldn't fathom the purpose of the Ocean's Forge, but its existence hinted at a connection between the industrial world and the mysterious force that governed the Iron Waves. Determined to unravel the secrets, Rowan delved into the intricacies of the Forge, deciphering its functions and decoding the language of its steam-powered mechanisms.

As he immersed himself in the exploration, Rowan became aware of a subtle shift in the underwater currents. Whispers of an ancient legend—the tale of the Ocean's Keeper—reverberated through the cavern. The Keeper, it was said, was a guardian of the Iron Waves, entrusted with maintaining the delicate balance between the industrial might of Steamport and the natural rhythms of the ocean.

Rowan's encounters with the Ocean's Keeper were ethereal as if he communed with a force that transcended time. Through visions and shared moments, he glimpsed the Keeper's role in guiding the surfers who dared to ride the Iron Waves. The underwater world, once a silent observer, now unfolded its stories, intertwining the destinies of those who navigated its depths.

As Rowan resurfaced from the hidden realms, he carried with him not only the knowledge of the Ocean's Forge but a profound connection to the ancient force that governed the Iron Waves. The discovery opened a new chapter in the subculture of steam-powered surfing, where surfers became not just riders of waves but guardians of a delicate equilibrium.

The return to the surface marked the beginning of a transformative journey for Rowan. The Iron Waves, once a canvas for his audacious maneuvers, now held a deeper significance. The surfing competitions, while exhilarating, became a means to share the wisdom he had gained from the hidden depths. The subculture once centered around the thrill of industrial surfing

As Rowan delved deeper into the intricate dance between the industrial world and the mysteries of the Iron Waves, he found himself increasingly drawn to the enigmatic force that governed the ocean's pulse—the Ocean's Keeper. The visions and shared moments with the Keeper became more frequent, blurring the lines between reality and the ethereal.

The whispers of ancient legends echoed through Rowan's mind, urging him to seek out the Keeper in the heart of the Iron Waves. A profound sense of destiny propelled him forward, guiding his surfboard through the familiar tumult of the industrial ocean. The subculture that once revelled in the thrill of steam-powered surfing now watched in awe as Rowan embarked on a journey that transcended the boundaries of man and machine.

The Iron Waves, stirred by an unseen force, seemed to guide Rowan towards an uncharted destination. The ocean's currents whispered secrets, and the steam-powered mechanisms of his surfboard responded to the harmonies of an ancient song. The convergence of man, machine, and nature reached its pinnacle as Rowan approached the epicentre of the Iron Waves.

In the heart of the tumultuous sea, a colossal whirlpool manifested—a gateway between the surface world and the submerged realms. The Ocean's Keeper, a spectral figure surrounded by the luminescent glow of underwater flora, emerged from the depths. Rowan, in awe of the entity that had guided his journey, felt a profound connection to the Keeper's silent wisdom.

As the Keeper extended a spectral hand, Rowan understood that his destiny was intertwined with the ancient force. The Iron Waves, once a canvas for daring feats, now beckoned him to become a guardian—a Keeper of the delicate equilibrium between industry and nature. The surfers who had once admired Rowan's prowess now witnessed his transformation into a figure shrouded in the mysteries of the ocean.

As Rowan embraced his role as the Ocean's Keeper, the Iron Waves responded with a symphony of steam-powered harmonies. The industrial sea, once turbulent and chaotic, now yielded to a rhythm that echoed the heartbeat of the ocean. The surfers of Steamport, inspired by Rowan's journey, began to recognize the fragile balance they needed to maintain.

However, this newfound harmony came at a price. Rowan, now tethered to the Keeper's ethereal essence, found himself caught between two worlds. His physical presence on the surface became fleeting, as the call of the Iron Waves compelled him to immerse himself in the ocean's depths. The surfers, torn between awe and apprehension, witnessed Rowan's transformation into a spectral figure—a guardian whose very existence was tied to the equilibrium he sought to preserve.

As Rowan's connection to the surface world weakened, a sense of isolation gripped his heart. The surfers, who once celebrated him as a legend, now watched from the shoreline as he faded into the luminescent embrace of the Iron Waves. The once-thriving subculture of steam-powered surfing began to wane, its vibrancy replaced by a sombre acknowledgment of the sacrifices made in the pursuit of harmony.

In the final act of his journey, Rowan faced the realization that the delicate equilibrium he sought to maintain required the ultimate sacrifice. The Ocean's Keeper, a silent witness to the ebb and flow of civilizations, conveyed a solemn truth—his existence was now tethered to the ocean's pulse, his identity forever intertwined with the Iron Waves

Printed in Great Britain
by Amazon